WICKED Valentine

A HOLIDAY BILLIONAIRE ROMANCE

ANASTASIA DEAN

ISBN:

E-book: 978-1-968095-05-5

Paperback: 978-1-968095-06-2

Edited By: Earley Editing

Cover Designer: Coffin Print Designs

For the Valentine's Day haters. This one's for you.

AUTHOR'S NOTE

This book contains elements of:

- Cam girl work / virtual sex work
- Explicit sexual scenes
- Workplace power and relationship dynamics

Please make sure you are protecting your mental health. If you need more information, send me a message on any of my socials. Otherwise, happy reading!

CHAPTER 1

CUPID CAN SUCK IT

Lety

The next person who walks in carrying a bouquet of roses that costs more than my rent is getting my high heel shoved up their ass. Starting with that bitch Melanie who has sauntered by not once, not twice, but *three* times holding an ugly ass vase with flowers from her overseas boyfriend. A boyfriend I'm almost certain doesn't exist since she never seems to have pictures of them together, despite being so *in love*.

The worst, though, are the flowers that come with a singing telegram. Who even knew that was still a thing? Because I certainly didn't, and after the third rendition of L-O-V-E, I was about ready to fling myself into oncoming traffic.

Needless to say, I fucking hate Valentine's Day.

I would have taken the day off if I remembered, but the last few weeks have been unusually busy for the office. One of the big boss lawyers, Elias, cut back on office hours to spend more time with his wife, leaving his secretary scrambling to reschedule. Since my boss, César, is his firm partner, I've been roped into rescheduling meetings and moving clients around to help ease the load of the other secretary.

Which is fine, I guess. It's not necessarily hard work, just frustrating. Especially when calendars are looking more like a color-by-number rather than a schedule, leaving it almost impossible to add a new workload onto another lawyer's plate. César needs to hire another lawyer or two, but his schedule barely allows him time to piss these days. I should know, since I schedule everything for him.

There's a knock on my door, and I snap my head up, expecting to see another flower delivery, but standing at my open door is Kase, Elias's secretary, leaning against the doorframe. He's sucking on a heart-shaped lollipop. Of course. "Lety, do you have a second?"

No.

"Of course." I give him my best customer service smile, closing my laptop. "What do you need?"

Kase walks in and perches his ass on the edge of my desk, nearly knocking over my bowl of mints. I try not to scowl at him, because I'm not trying to start an office rivalry, and I actually do like Kase. I'm just irritated with all the lovey-dovey shit and cupid nonsense. Just call me the Grinch of Valentine's Day.

"We got a problem," he tells me. I sigh because it feels like we *always* have a problem these days. "The contractor for the winter expansion project needs to reschedule his meeting."

"Okay, that's not too bad. When does he want to meet with César?"

"Next Wednesday."

I take that back. "Fuck." I quickly open my laptop again and immediately pull up César's schedule. I know what I'll find before I see it, but the calendar shows no signs of wiggle room.

"There's no way he can meet with the contractor on Wednesday. Can't he do another day? I might be able to schedule him for the following Monday."

"Nope," Kase says, popping his lips on the "p." "He'll also be booked up for the next two months, so unless César is okay with pushing back his plans to expand the firm, someone's gotta figure out something. That someone is you, doll." Kase winks at me before pushing himself off my desk to head out. "Good luck!" he calls over his shoulder before bolting out.

Coward.

I groan, a tension headache coming on. Good thing this job has excellent healthcare or else this stress wouldn't be worth it. Besides, tonight I'll take out all my frustration during my show. It's my little wicked secret—something that allows me to take ownership of my sexuality and ease the stress from the day. Plus, taking money from men is my favorite pastime.

I just have to get through another four hours and a quick meeting with my boss before I can think about my nighttime job. Then I can spend Valentine's Day doing what I love most.

Myself.

Pushing up from my pink, padded chair, I grab my laptop. César is in between meetings now, which gives me a short window of opportunity to speak with him before his next client. After adjusting my skirt that's ridden up to an almost scandalous level, I head toward my boss's office.

Fucking Melanie is still talking about her pretend

boyfriend as I pass her, and I do my best not to roll my eyes. I'm tempted to "accidentally" swipe my hand across her desk and knock down her gaudy arrangement of flowers, but I'm a proper lady, so I don't.

I just think about doing it. Repeatedly.

César's office is on the third-story. My heels aren't made for stairs, so I take the elevator, ignoring the judging looks all chubby people get when they opt for the elevator. If they want to be miserable and huff and puff up the stairs, they can have at it. I hold my head a little higher when the doors finally open, and I step inside.

Soft elevator music plays—thankfully not a love song—when I enter and select his floor. I tap my manicured nail against my laptop, checking my watch. Ten minutes until César's next appointment. I'll need to be quick.

When the doors open again, I step into the floor's silence. Gracie, another receptionist, peeks her head up from her desk and offers me a smile. "Lety, how's it going down under?"

"Oh, you know. It's like cupid threw up all over the place. Is César in his office?" He should be, but I ask anyway in case he ran off to the bathroom or went in search of something to eat.

Gracie nods. "He is. His next clients are here, so he'll be busy soon. I'd hurry if you need to talk with him."

"This will only take a minute," I assure, walking past her desk to the double set of mahogany doors. I knock once, but don't wait for a response before barging in. The Lety who started this job last year would have never had the guts to simply walk in uninvited, but a year in this firm has hardened me. There's only one way to get what you want here, and it's not hiding behind nerves.

César is leaning over his desk, completely absorbed in

whatever email has his attention. His jacket's open and his sleeves are pushed up just enough to show the edge of a tattoo winding up his forearm. The suit clings to him like it was directly sewn on, top buttons undone to tease a hint of his chest.

He's unreadable, jaw tense, with one hand braced against the desk while the other rubs his mouth like he's trying not to say something out loud. The light from his monitor casts shadows across his chest, catching on the pendant that rests right between his pecs. It shouldn't look that good. *He* shouldn't look that good.

I let my gaze linger for half a second too long before snapping myself out of it. Yes, he's attractive. Stupidly so. The kind of man who ruins lives with a smirk and knows it. But I'm not here for that. I'm here to work, get my shit done, and definitely not drool over my boss. No matter how annoyingly perfect he looks at all times.

"Mr. Estrada." My voice carries in the room, reverberating off the windows. He raises a brow, surprised to see me in his office, as if he didn't hear my big entrance. I swear this man has no idea of the things happening around him when he's lost in work.

"Miss Zavala," he says in that gravely tone of his that has probably soaked more panties than he knows. It's not just that my boss is hot as fuck, it's that he knows he's hot as fuck and uses that to his advantage.

César sits back in his chair, arms moving to rest behind his head. His shirt pulls taunt against his chest, showcasing the muscles he's worked hard for at the gym. Or from fucking half the female population. Not certain which one. A lazy smile pulls at the corner of his lips. "What can I do for you?"

His words remind me why I'm here, and it's certainly

not to drool over my boss. Unlike half the staff here, I've made it my mission not to throw myself at César in a desperate attempt to gain his favor. That's more than I can say for the other women, and a few men, at the office. They are all wasting their time, though. César has never dated anyone he's worked with in the year I've been here. Probably afraid it would complicate things too much.

"This is about the contractor," I say, bracing for his frustration. "He needs to reschedule the meeting; except the only time he can reschedule is for next Wednesday."

"That shouldn't be a problem," he says, and I have to stop myself from gritting my teeth. Of course he hasn't checked his schedule. Why would he when he has worker bees like me to run it for him?

"Well, it actually is a problem because you have no availability on Wednesday." I do my best to keep the annoyance out of my voice, but it still bleeds through. "And I mean none. You don't even have time to piss."

César raises a brow, and my cheeks instantly flush. Why the fuck would I bring up his bathroom breaks? It's just the first thing to pop into my mind to show just how stacked his Wednesday calendar is and the problem we're facing.

"No time to piss, eh? You're working me like a damn dog, Miss Zavala." Again with that damn smile. Only this time, there's lingering fatigue hidden behind it. The man is working too damn much, having picked up the slack from Mr. Ayala. Before then, César had a strict four-day work-week policy, which I know he's itching to get back to.

With a sigh, César untangles his hands from behind his head and runs his fingers through his gelled, black hair. After a brief pause of being lost in thought, his deep brown eyes bore into me. "You're certain there's no time?"

Instead of answering, I open the lid of my laptop and pull up his calendar and march my ass to his side. "You're welcome to look for yourself," I say, and hand him the laptop, which he takes. His brows knit tightly together as he quickly scans, seeing for himself the clusterfuck that is his calendar.

"Fuck," he murmurs under his breath. I probably was not meant to hear. He runs a finger over each time block, mumbling incoherently to himself. After a moment of silent deliberation, he says, "Schedule him for noon, and push everyone else back an hour."

Now it's my turn to raise a brow. "Really? That has you at the office from six in the morning to nearly seven at night."

"Worried about me, Miss Zavala?" He grins, cheekily, brushing off the fact his days just went from sucky to torturously long.

"More so worried about myself and the demands you'll make from lack of sleep."

His answering laugh definitely doesn't make me squeeze my thighs together or send a pleasurable shiver down my spine.

Get your shit together, Lety! You are on a strict no man diet.

And even if I wasn't, I wouldn't be going after my boss.

César hands me back my laptop, but then accidentally knocks over a stack of papers on his desk in the process. Without thinking, I bend over and snatch them off the ground. It's not until I stand up that I realize I just had my whole ass in César's face. My skirt isn't indecent, but I can't make that same promise when I'm bent over for the world to see.

Fuck me.

Maybe he didn't notice. He definitely doesn't make a

comment, but his eyes trail over every curve of my body before reaching my outstretched hand.

"Thank you."

Is it just me or did his voice grow deeper? His hands brush mine when he takes the stack of papers, sending a shockwave through my body.

I tell myself it has nothing to do with César and all to do with my show tonight and finally letting off enough steam so I'm not a horny mess. I blame the day, too. Fuck Cupid and fuck love.

"Anyway," I say when I realize we are both just standing there like idiots. I take my laptop back from him, closing it and holding it to my chest like a protective barrier between us. "I'll go switch up the schedule and send you a message when it's updated."

Not waiting for a response and needing to put as much distance between César and myself as possible, I turn on my heels and make a beeline for the door.

But I'm not fast enough.

Before I can leave, he calls out, "Oh, and Miss Zavala?"

I pause, angling my body toward him. "Yes?"

"Happy Valentine's Day." Aware of my not-so-hidden disdain for Valentine's Day, the bastard smirks. It takes everything in me not to reply with a bitchy comment, even though I desperately want to.

"It's the merriest day of the year!" I say with fake enthusiasm.

"Pretty sure that's Christmas."

"Whatever," I mumble, tossing my hair over my shoulder, resuming my exit. I swear I hear his deep baritone laughter follow me down the hallway.

CHAPTER 2
HER SECRET SHOW

César

It's Valentine's Day and I'm sitting at home, two glasses of whiskey deep, without a woman by my side. I don't fucking care at this point. Valentine's Day is my favorite time of the year. An excuse to spoil my date with cheap chocolate and not-so-cheap flowers. We'd share a night of passion, because what was Valentine's Day for if not hot, rough sex? And then we'd part ways—usually on amicable terms—and the cycle would start anew next year.

Women are my favorite indulgence. Spoiling them. Fucking them. Talking with them. It didn't matter. My friend and firm partner, Elias, always made fun of me and called me a playboy, but that shit is the furthest thing from the truth. Playboys don't respect women and are just there for some ass. Not me. I want every part a woman will give me. Her hopes, dreams, fears. I fucking thrive on that shit.

It's just the commitment I'm not good at.

I've never cheated on anyone. I'm not that type of

man. I've also never been with anyone long enough to cheat on them, which is what I prefer. My interests are fleeting, and no woman has ever stayed on my mind for long.

The only reason I'm not at some overpriced three Michelin star restaurant is because I've been working like a damn dog. My calendar is packed, filled with back-to-back meetings, since Elias decided to become a better husband and spend more time with his wife. I think that asshole is in Mexico on some beach.

Can't help but hate him a little.

I finish my third glass of whiskey just as a notification buzzes my phone. A reminder flashes across the screen—five minutes until my show starts. If I have to miss out on my favorite holiday, then damn it, I'm going to enjoy it in other ways. I grab my personal laptop and power it on. The website is already saved in my favorites. As soon as I log in, a banner pops up across the screen, proudly declaring me CurvyBabe's top supporter once again. Just like I've been for the last three months.

I loosen my tie, unbuttoning my shirt before nestling back into my couch, getting comfortable. My cock already knows what's about to happen and twitches in my pants. It's been too damn long since I've sunk myself into tight pussy, I'm certain I'm going through withdrawals. Until I get my personal life back, CurvyBabe is my only outlet.

The video feed starts up with a two-minute countdown for tonight's live event. Before I'm too far gone in my horny thoughts, I send a generous tip, gaining the "top contributor" badge instantly. A widget in the corner of the screen counts the amount of people joining in on the live and it quickly surpasses over one thousand people. I take solace in knowing I'm not the only bastard spending Valentine's Day alone.

Me—and probably the entire chat—watch in anticipation as the countdown gets to its last five seconds. The moment it hits one, the screen goes dark. Before disappointment can settle in, the screen flashes again, and this time, *she's* here. CurvyBabe. A masquerade mask covers her face, concealing most of her identity.

She's wearing this fiery-red lace number that barely counts as clothing. It clings to her curves like a second skin, cut low enough to showcase the swell of her breasts. A keyhole slit teases a glimpse of skin right between them. Thin straps wrap around her shoulders, delicate but firm, like the lingerie was made to be slowly undone.

My gaze dips lower. The bodysuit hugs her waist and hips like a damn dream, sheer panels and lace revealing more than they hide. There are little ruffles at her hips, and long garter straps trail down her thighs like an invitation. She's paired it with matching red thigh-highs, and suddenly I can't think straight.

She shifts slightly, running a hand through her hair like she owns the room—and hell, she does. My blood heats instantly. Every nerve lights up. That lingerie wasn't made to be worn. It was made to be worshipped—just like her— and ripped off.

Fuck.

My mouth is dry. She hasn't even said a word yet, and I already know I'm screwed. My cock swells at the sight of her. Soft, sultry music plays in the background, adding to the ambiance of her small room with nothing but a twin sized bed.

"Happy Valentine's Day," she purrs, a seductress in her own right. Her voice drips like honey. She never speaks much. She doesn't have to. Her body does all the talking for her.

I drink her in like a fine wine. Her soft belly, wide hips, and thighs that could send a lesser man into a coma. Although most of the comments are praising and complimenting her body, there are a few unhinged ones as well.

> FATTIE.
> FUCKING GROSS.
> NO PERSON SHOULD BE THAT BIG.

I see red. Fuckers like that are only brave behind a screen and thrive in anonymity. Their tiny dicks could never win over a woman like CurvyBabe, so they throw their little tantrums online to feel superior. It's truly pathetic, but their viewership and comments give her money, so they are just inadvertently helping her. Still, I report their comments in the hope it's enough to get them banned.

Reporting the comments distract me so much that I almost miss the sultry moans coming from the video. My gaze snaps up in time to see CurvyBabe fondle herself. She squeezes her large breast between her hands, letting her head fall back. More moans escape her lips, and they can only be compared to the sound of a siren. My cock hardens painfully in my pants, restricted by the tight fabric.

I undo the top of my pants to ease the pressure. But it's not enough, and I don't stand a chance.

I pull on the zipper, nearly hissing as my cock springs free from its confines. Half hard already, I wrap my hand around my shaft, pumping it up and down with a groan. My eyelids threaten to close, but I can't miss a second of the show. Of *her*.

One manicured hand—red nails that match her

lingerie perfectly—sneaks down between her legs. I hadn't noticed before, but it's evident now. An open slit stretches across her crotch, allowing her fingers to dip in easily. The moment her finger finds her clit, she gasps, and I imagine every viewer moaning alongside her.

Her pussy is still mostly covered, but we get enough of a tease to hang on to her every action. I don't miss the way her lips part in a silent gasp as she presses a finger inside herself, moving it in and out in a slow, rhythmic motion.

I follow her pace, stroking my cock painfully slowly. It's sweet torture. I both hate and love it, needing more, but not wanting this to end too quickly.

CurvyBabe commands the camera, having every bastard salivating at their screen. She sits back on the bed and spreads her legs wide. The fabric of her lingerie pulls taut over her center, the slit opening to expose the pretty pink of her pussy. And fuck if it isn't the hottest thing I've seen. An involuntary groan leaves my lips as I squeeze my cock, pretending my hand is her pussy.

I really need to get fucking laid.

She adds a second finger into her needy cunt, and her sultry moans grow louder. This is her favorite way to get started, slowly fucking herself with her fingers and coming all over them. She moves to toys next. I've watched far too many of her videos not to know her pattern, and even though it's predictable, I still come hard every time. This goddess of a woman has an effect over me like no other, and she doesn't even know who I am. Hell, I don't even know who she is. Not really.

When her fingers move faster, I match her pace with my hand. Soon my moans mix with hers as I picture myself sheathing my cock inside her cunt and fucking her within an inch of her life. Because I'm a damn gentleman, I'd make sure she came first, drawing out every ounce of pleasure until she begged for me to stop. And even then, I would coax another one out of her before spilling my cum so deep inside of her that I'll forever be etched on her body.

Pressure builds in my lower abdomen, growing more intense with each stroke of my hand. Precum gathers at my tip, as if in preparation to explode for her at any minute. The pressure moves from my abdomen down, locking my body up. It won't be long now; this woman can unwind me without even touching me.

"Fuck," she moans into the camera, cheeks flushed and her fingers moving at a punishing pace. Wetness pools between her thighs, making her fingers slide in easily. I imagine myself pumping in and out of her, hard and fast. The moans she would make for me, how her body would wither under mine, and how we would come undone together.

The last thought pushes me over the edge. I groan, squeezing my cock as ropes of cum spurts on my stomach. CurvyBabe screams out, finding her own orgasm, and my spent cock twitches upon seeing her finish.

At the end, I'm left satisfied, with mild disappointment tainting my post orgasm bliss. Reality settles in, and I remember I'm alone. Alone on Valentine's Day and alone in life while those around me have been married and settled for some time.

I don't know if that's the life I want, but I want *something*. Or maybe that's just my horniness talking, and I'll get out of this funk after I'm buried to the hilt in someone's pussy.

"I think it's time to change positions," CurvyBabe purrs, drawing my attention back to the screen.

My social life problems can wait. For now, I'll live in this bubble of pleasure.

CurvyBabe moves to her hands and knees, arching her back just enough to tilt her hips up, positioning herself perfectly within the camera frame. That ass—*that* fucking ass—has been the downfall of my bank account. Round, soft, and sinful, it bounces slightly with every small shift she makes. She moves like she knows exactly what it does to me. I've dropped *so* much money just to see it again and again, to have her turn and show it off like it's a damn masterpiece, because it *is*. That ass has haunted my dreams, wrecked my focus at work, and still, it's never enough. I'd pay a thousand times over just to watch it move for me.

CurvyBabe starts talking, but her words are lost to me. I have a one-track mind with her ass on the screen, admiring every inch. And then I zero in on the tattoo on her lower back, just above her ass. It's a small, delicate piece. A butterfly with pink wings. I've seen it a hundred times before, but this time, it stirs up a memory. Foggy at first, like it's unsure if it wants to take form.

And then I remember.

My body freezes, locking up, and I'm certain the color drains from my face as if I've just seen a ghost.

But this is so much worse than a ghost.

So much fucking worse.

Because I've seen that tattoo before. Not just through a screen—but in my office. Just a few hours ago. She dropped some papers. Bent over to grab them. That slutty little skirt rode up her thighs, giving me a view I shouldn't have taken—but did, anyway. Her shirt shifted just enough to expose her lower back.

That's when I saw it.

A butterfly. Inked in delicate lines. Pink wings.

The same fucking tattoo.

Lety Zavala is CurvyBabe.

How the fuck am I supposed to face my secretary now?

There's a small possibility that these women just have the same tattoo, but the more I look at CurvyBabe, the more I see the similarities between them. Same black hair that hangs nearly to her ass, curly and full. Those same pouty lips I've dreamed about on more than one occasion.

How could I not have seen it before? The truth is so obvious as it stares me in the face, mocking me with my own stupidity. My number-one rule has always been to never get involved with an employee, no matter how tempting.

And Lety is so fucking tempting—making me contemplate breaking my own rules. It's been easy to ignore her and pretend that my body doesn't react each time that perky ass walks by my door with those wicked high heels.

Now that I know this information, what the fuck do I do with it?

I know one thing for certain: Lety Zavala has become my new obsession.

And this time, I don't think I want to ignore my need for her. Maybe it's time to break all the rules.

CHAPTER 3
OFFICE GAMES

Lety

I think I'm getting fired.

César has gone out of his way not to talk to me, going as far as denying my phone calls, only to send a quickly worded email to communicate with me. It doesn't take much to read between the lines that my boss is unhappy. The question I'm left with is what the fuck did I do?

Nothing has changed. These last two weeks, I have made his appointments as normal, juggled his schedule, met with his clients, and all the other small admin tasks that come across my desk. Then again, maybe he's frustrated that nothing has changed. Like he expects me to get better at my job. Which is a load of shit, because I'm already damn good at what I do. I'm timely, efficient, and extremely organized. I don't drop the ball, and that's a lot more than I can say about the other admins and secretaries here. I don't see how I could be any better at what I do.

It got even worse when César sent Melanie and Kase to deliver messages he could've given me over a quick call. That's not like him—he's never shut me out like this before. Normally, he makes a point to greet everyone in the building each morning, always stopping by my little office for five minutes to shoot the shit and I'd fill him in on his day. But now? He hasn't approached me once in the last two weeks. Not a word. And I can't shake the feeling that something's seriously wrong.

Despite these turbulent weeks, I've stayed focused on the work. It seems to pile up daily at this point, and I'll be relieved when the expansion is finally complete. César and Elias can hire more people then. I've been in back-to-back meetings today, not even having a moment to work on the mountain of paperwork piling up on my desk.

Looks like tonight is going to be a long day in the office, and thankfully, I have no scheduled shows that would conflict with my day job.

Being a camgirl has brought in a lot of confidence—and money. I know people say this all the time, but I truly don't do it for the money. Though it is nice—I won't lie about that. However, I enjoy the power it brings me. The way I can command an entire audience, who have all paid to watch me—it's a big boost to my self-esteem. Half of these men wouldn't ever admit to liking bigger girls in real life, but they certainly eat it up in private.

So, if I lost this job, I wouldn't be completely without pay. But the benefits here are great, and the income is more than I would get anywhere else. Plus, I actually like my job. I don't plan on being a camgirl for the rest of my life, and I don't want to rely on it to be my main source of income. It's a job, sure, but it's also a fun way for me to distress, and I don't want that feeling to go away by making it my sole source of income. I prefer it being more of a hobby, so it doesn't lose its sexy appeal.

By the time I finish with the first stack of paperwork, the office has cleared out. The room is dark, except for the dim light filtering in through the windows. The sun is setting quickly, bathing the room in a soft honey glow. The janitorial team has started their nightly routine, and I wave at Mr. Anderson, the head janitor for our floor. I've gotten to know him a bit over the last few weeks because of the late nights. He waves back with a cheerful smile before getting back to work.

I turn back to the stack of papers on my desk. One page leads to another, and soon I'm in the zone—focused, tuned out from the world around me. The hum of the office, the occasional voices in the hallway, all fades away as I immerse myself in the reports. Time slips by unnoticed. It isn't until my eyes strain against the dim light that I realize the sun has set, stealing away the only natural light in the room. I reach up and flip on the desk lamp, barely pausing before diving back in. Just as I reach for the next report, something brushes my shoulder. I scream like I'm the lead actor in a horror film and shoot out of my chair, heart pounding.

I whirl, hand on my chest to see what touched me. Leaning against my door, with an amused smile on his face, is César. I freeze, both shocked and terrified to see him here. I should have known he'd be here just as late, but considering he's kept me at arm's-length these past two weeks, I forgot he was in the building.

"Have you ever heard of knocking?" I snap, unable to hide my embarrassment from the overreaction. Part of me realizes I shouldn't be snapping at the man who holds my future in the palm of his hands and signs my check, but I've never been good at hiding my emotions.

"I did. Multiple times," he muses, pushing off the door, moving into my closet-sized office. The space suddenly feels suffocating with César's large body taking up the room. We're so close I can smell the spearmint from his aftershave.

"You...did?"

"Mm-hmm." He perches on the edge of my desk. "Saw that you were still here and wondered why you'd be here this late."

"I could ask you the same question."

"Could you?" He raises a brow. "And here I thought you managed my calendar."

"Oh, so you're acknowledging me personally for the work I do? And here *I* thought you only did that through your other employees." I can't keep the bitterness out of my voice. Because the truth is, I'm hurt. I hate that I'm coming to work each day, nervous it's going to be my last. I hate the added stress put on an already stressful job.

The look of bewilderment on César's face takes me by surprise. Which only further confuses me. "Did you come in here to fire me? Because if you are, just say it already."

"Fire you?" His eyes go comically wide. It would be funny if it wasn't such a serious topic. "Why the fuck would I fire you?"

"Because..." All the pent-up rage leaves me in an instant, leaving me feeling foolish. Maybe I was reading into things that weren't there? I've seen his schedule. Hell, I run his schedule, so I know how busy he's been. He's doing all he can to keep afloat. So am I.

"I'm sorry," I say after an awkward pause. "I don't know

what I was thinking. I guess we've all been under a great amount of stress."

César sighs, running a hand through his hair. I can't help but stare at how much his shirt strains, showing off the muscles he's hiding underneath. "No, I'm sorry. I've been preoccupied. You thought I was going to fire you this whole time?"

My face flushes, and I nod, not trusting my voice.

César mutters a low string of Spanish curses and storms around my desk. Before I can react, he's in front of me—his body pressing in, backing me against the wall. My breath catches as his chest brushes mine, solid and unyielding. This is far from appropriate, but I can't bring myself to care.

"You are my best damn employee," he growls, voice rough with emotion. "I'm not losing you." His eyes burn into mine, fierce and unwavering. "If you ever feel like this again—like you don't matter—you come to me. You tell me. Because *you*"—his hand comes up, fingers skimming my jaw in a phantom touch—"are too damn important to me to be walking around thinking I don't want you."

His voice dips lower, husky now. His eyes dip down to my chest, and I swear his pupils dilate. "Because I do. Maybe more than I should. And your happiness is important to me."

His words slam into me, stealing the breath from my lungs. My body reacts on its own accord, arching closer to him. My nipples pebble, almost painfully so. Heat rushes between my legs. *Get yourself together. This is your fucking boss! You've sworn off men, too, remember?*

I remember. I just can't seem to get my vagina to remember that. César and I walk a precarious line. At this moment, I don't feel like his employee. He licks his lips, and it takes everything in me not to close the space between us and kiss him until I consume every part of him.

It would be wrong. Very wrong.

And yet the temptation is nearly impossible to ignore. With the air thick with heat, my body is ready to surrender to something raw.

I'm seconds from leaning in when César suddenly steps back. The distance between us hits me like a bucket of ice water, shocking me back to reality.

He stands there, calm and composed, like nothing just happened. Like the tension crackling between us was entirely one-sided and he didn't just say he wanted me. I blink, stunned, my heart still racing. Did I imagine it? That electric pull, the way his eyes darkened, the way the world seemed to fall away? Or is my overtired mind conjuring fantasies I shouldn't be having about my boss?

"You should go home, Lety. It's getting late," he says. Lety. Not Miss Zavala. He speaks my name like a gentle caress that leaves me feeling warm all over again. It also gives me whiplash. Like one minute, I think he wants me and the next, he's cold and distant.

"I can't," I manage to say, somehow finding my voice. "I have reports I need to go through tonight."

César stops and turns to look at the stack of papers on my desk. Without another word, he leaves, and I'm more confused than ever. A moment later, something squeaks against the tile. César comes back, pulling an office chair, which he parks right in front of my desk. To my amazement—and horror—he takes a seat, grabbing the top report. "Then we better get to work."

"Oh, I don't need your help—"

"I didn't ask if you needed my help," he replies, head

bowed as he pretends to be fascinated by whatever is in the report. "Besides, I'm not leaving you alone in this building and letting you walk to your car at night by yourself."

Again, he steals my ability to speak, which is really fucking annoying because I always have something to say. Instead, I sit my ass down at my desk, peering over at him like that will somehow help me make sense of the situation.

"We could be here late," I say in hopes it will persuade him to leave. "Don't you have anything you need to do? A date or a bar you want to go to?"

"A bar?" He smirks. "Do I look like I'm in my twenties?" It's not lost on me he mentioned nothing about a date. "No, Lety, I think I would rather be here."

"But—"

"What about dinner?" He completely ignores me and pulls out his phone. "You like those street tacos from Las Trancas, don't you?"

"I do ..." I confirm, suspiciously. "But how did you know that?"

"Because you ordered it twice last week. You also mentioned it to me awhile back."

I don't ever remember talking about places I like to eat, but he somehow pinpointed my favorite place in town —a small, local food truck ran by the sweetest family. My face heats at the thought of César knowing how many times I've ordered food. A girl's gotta eat, but a girl hates to cook.

"Fine, but I'll pay for my half. I want—"

"Carnitas. And no, you won't pay for shit."

I'm getting really tired of this man talking over me, but I'm also not going to argue if he wants to spend his money on me. I'm not going to try to convince him otherwise. I make a living out of taking money from men.

"Okay, I suppose if you're going to feed me, you can also help me with the reports. They're all for you anyway." I settle in my spot, rolling my head from side to side, and grab the next report.

César's lips curve into a slow, confident smile. "I'll feed you whenever you want. As long as I'm the only one buying you food."

The words hit me like a spark, warm and confusing all at once. I open my mouth to ask him what he means. If he's flirting, staking some kind of claim, or just being his usual charming self, but before I can get a single word out, he's already returned his attention to his phone. The sudden shift leaves me sitting there, blinking, my mind spinning with questions.

Does he see me that way? Was that a joke, or something more? Why do I even care?

I replay his voice in my head, trying to decode the tone, the look in his eyes, the timing of it all. But I get nothing—no clues, no certainty. Just a lingering heat in my chest and a million thoughts I can't quite stitch together.

And as the silence stretches between us, I realize something dangerous is beginning to bloom.

And I have no idea what to do about it.

CHAPTER 4

LATE NIGHTS AND
DARK SECRETS

Lety

The days pass in a blur of meetings, paperwork, and spreadsheets. I'm exhausted by the time I leave the office—late, of course. César has stayed with me every night, either working silently by my desk, or feeding me dinner from another one of my favorite food trucks. By the third day, it hit me that César never stays late to work on his own tasks. He only sticks around to help me with mine. Which led me to believe he was there for me...but why?

As much as I hated to admit it, I liked the attention and knowing César cared about my safety.

Because of the long days at the office, I've completely ignored my DesireDen account. I've popped on a few times to respond to comments and messages, and posted a few half-dressed selfies, but that's all I've had the energy for. I've started to miss my live shows—and, of course, the amazing orgasms that come with preforming—so I've vowed to make time for a live show on DesireDen. Judging by the reaction from my audience when I posted I'd have a show tonight, they had missed my performances as well.

However, in order to get ready for tonight, I had to call in sick for work. The people-pleaser in me felt bad for leaving César without help, but his response had been... unexpected after my text.

I'm sending over lunch. Take it easy and don't you dare open your work computer.

I won't.

Good girl.

Good girl? The fucking man is going to be the death of me. Does he even know what he said and the effect it has on women? He has to. That asshole.

True to his word, César sends a small feast that could feed a family of five, as well as dessert, since he knows I have a sweet tooth.

"Oh, César, the man you are," I murmur between bites of picadillo. Once again, he knows exactly what I would order, as if he's been secretly studying me for months. I don't know if I should be flattered or concerned. I'm leaning toward the former, though.

Pushing all thoughts of my boss out of my mind, I get ready for my live, opting to wear the new angel lingerie costume I bought. Seems fitting since I'm going with a good girl theme—totally not inspired by César at all. Just a happy coincidence.

I also don't think about César when I start the camera, my boobs filling the screen. I watch as the number of viewers rises to levels I haven't seen in a while. I must have been away longer than I thought.

I don't think of César when I take my vibrator out from the nightside table.

I definitely don't think of him when I place it against my clit, letting the vibrations create undeniable pleasure.

And I don't think about him when I come on my fingers. His brown eyes aren't looking back at me when I close my eyes.

I don't think about it because it would be highly inappropriate of me to get off on the thoughts of my boss.

Messages flood my inbox the moment I end the short livestream, right after promising a private session to the top bidder. Notifications chime in one after another, and I glance at my DesireDen wallet. My jaw nearly drops. The balance leaps from a few hundred to several thousand in seconds, skyrocketing the moment a familiar username appears: DineroDaddy.

I shouldn't be surprised. He's been my top contributor for months now, always first to tip, first to comment, and first to slide into my DMs. Of course he'd win the private chat. His bid crushed the others without even trying. Still, there's a strange twist in my stomach when I think about how much he's sent me over time. Thousands. And tonight alone? Enough to make me blink twice.

I don't usually feel guilty about taking money from men who willingly hand it over. But there's something about DineroDaddy—something that makes me pause. Then again, with a name like that, I doubt he's hurting for cash, so I clamp the guilt deep down. This is my job, after all, and the money is given willingly.

CurvyBabe: *Hi, DineroDaddy. Looks like you are the top contributor again. You've won the private show. Just give me a minute to change into something cozier and I'll be back.*

I type out the message and hit send, my heart ticking just a little faster. From across the room, the red negligée hanging in my closet seems to beckon me—a barely-there lace bra, matching panties, and a sheer robe that leaves little to the imagination. I'm just about to stand to go slip it on when my phone buzzes. His reply makes me freeze mid-motion.

DineroDaddy: *No need, mi reina. I just want to talk.*

Talk? I nearly laugh at the absurdity of the request.

CurvyBabe: *You sure spent a lot of money just to talk. It won't take me long to slip into something you'd like and turn on my camera.*

DineroDaddy: *Tempting. So goddamned tempting. But I just want to talk to you.*

I've had odd requests in the past. People wanting to see my feet, wanting to see me go to the bathroom, and one that wanted me to dress up as a cat. Not a sexy cat, no, a full-on cat costume. But no one has ever just wanted to talk. It was odd...yet refreshing.

CurvyBabe: *Okay, Daddy. What do you want to talk about?*

DineroDaddy: *Fuck, maybe I do want to hear you call me Daddy on camera.*

CurvyBabe: *Still time to change your mind...*

DineroDaddy: *You are tempting, mi reina. So damn tempting, like a siren. But I'll stick with my original plan. Get to know you. Tell me anything about you.*

I can't help the wave of disappointment that washes over me. Until I remember how much he's spending just to *talk*, then I perk right back up. Still, I have to carefully navigate this conversation because keeping my identity a secret is important to me.

CurvyBabe: *Well, I like to read. Usually books that will make my grandma roll over in her grave. And I also love superhero movies. For the aesthetics, of course.*

Thank God for spandex and hot asses. I mean, why else watch a superhero movie?

DineroDaddy: *Does your boyfriend make you watch those movies?*

I hesitate, rereading his message again. It's not uncommon for my viewers to ask about my personal life. They all want to know if my partner knows I pleasure myself for strangers online. As if a girl can't have a hobby without asking permission. I'm not certain this is information I want to divulge yet, so I play with him like a cat to a mouse.

CurvyBabe: *Bold of you to assume I have a boyfriend.*

DineroDaddy: *Girlfriend, then.*

I know he's fishing for information, and normally, I'd

steer the conversation somewhere else. I've always been careful about what I share, keeping parts of myself tucked away for the sake of privacy and safety. But with Dinero-Daddy, it feels different, since no one has ever just wanted to talk. I can't fully explain it, and I definitely can't justify it, but something about it has me lowering my guard.

Maybe it's the way he's consistently shown up—always at the top of my contributor list, always commenting, liking, engaging during lives like he's actually listening. His steady presence makes him feel like someone I know—someone who sees more of me than just the show. It's not something I feel with the others.

Again, I realize this is delusional and probably stupid, but feelings rarely make logical sense. And sometimes fighting those feelings takes too much energy to manage.

> **CurvyBabe:** *No girlfriend either. I prefer the single life and my freedom. I've had my share of bad relationships, and I'm perfectly content with being alone. Besides, a girlfriend who is a sex worker would intimidate most men. Don't you think?*

> **DineroDaddy:** *Seems to me you've dated weak men.*

Despite myself, I laugh. He's not wrong, but he didn't have to call me out like that. Damn. In my defense, my past boyfriends felt like knights in shining armor at the start of our relationships. But don't they always until they have to prove themselves worth your time?

> **CurvyBabe:** *Hence why I'm by myself, Daddy. I get to talk to sexy men like you and give myself amazing orgasms. Much better than being disappointed by a man who thinks three minutes is gold medal worthy.*

DineroDaddy: *How do you know I'm sexy?*

CurvyBabe: *You got big dick energy. That makes you sexy. Obviously.*

DineroDaddy: *Careful, mi reina. Keep talking like that and I will change my mind about that private show.*

I smirk at the screen, a familiar flutter stirring low in my belly again. Part of me still hopes for that private show. It would be fun. He has this way of toeing the line—flirty without being crude, dominant without being demanding. It's a rare combo in this line of work. Most men crash through boundaries like angry bulls, but not him. Dinero-Daddy is smooth with his words. Too damn smooth. Two can play that game, though.

CurvyBabe: *Then maybe I want you to change your mind.*

I send the message before I can overthink it, before I can remind myself that I don't actually know this man. Even if I feel like I do. That no matter how sweet or consistent he seems online, he's still a stranger. I was taught stranger danger in school, so I should know better. But something in me is leaning in, curious, maybe even reckless, and I'm letting the feeling lead me.

His typing bubble appears immediately, then disappears. Appears again. Whatever he's writing, he's rewriting. Thinking. Is his heart beating as fast as mine? God, I hope it is.

When his message finally lands, it's not what I expect.

DineroDaddy: *You ever think about settling down? Have the online persona and the romantic partner? Someone who respects and celebrates every part of you?*

I blink at the question. My throat tightens a little. It's not that I've never thought about it. Of course I have. But finding a partner that will accept this part of my life seems impossible. I refuse to choose between my work and a man. Perhaps that makes me selfish, but I don't care. I crave the thrill and validation cam life brings me. It's addictive in its own right. Not to mention how empowered I feel. Plus, this is my own creative outlet, and for now, it's where I want to put my energy into.

But no one's ever asked me that. Not like this. Not like they actually cared about the answer.

CurvyBabe: ***Sometimes.*** *But this life gives me freedom. I don't owe anyone shit. I get to feel sexually fulfilled.*

The dots appear again. Typing... stop... typing. My leg bounces with anticipation, a nervous habit I've never grown out of.

DineroDaddy: *And is that enough for you?*

My stomach twists as a mix of confusion and despair wash through me. I don't know why his question hits so hard. Maybe because no one's ever asked before. I love my job. But...is it enough?

Deep down, I'm not certain it is because part of me wants this life, but the other part of me wants a life with a partner to cuddle up with at night. And I can't fathom having both.

I lean back in my chair, eyes scanning over his message again and again, like it might mean something more than it says. Like he knows something about me I haven't told him.

And maybe that's what unsettles me most. How seen I feel. Fuck this bastard.

CurvyBabe: *You talk like a man who's got answers.*

DineroDaddy: *Maybe I've lived a little. Loved enough women to know they deserve better.*

CurvyBabe: *Sounds like player behavior.*

DineroDaddy: *Touché. But I meant it. I see you, mi reina. Not just the performance. You.*

My breath hitches. My fingers glide over the keyboard, at a loss of what to say next.

I should end the chat. Log off. Tell him I'm tired, make up an excuse—hell, even pretend my Wi-Fi dropped. But I don't, because I can't. I don't want to. Instead, I type something that feels a little too raw.

CurvyBabe: *Sometimes I wish I could run away to a cabin and be in my own little world. Just me and someone I love. You keep saying you see me, but I don't even know what you look like. Or anything about you.*

It's my version of fishing. A way to pull back the curtain without fully yanking it down. It's wrong and opens up far too much shit that I'm not prepared to face yet. Or ever.

His reply comes slower this time.

DineroDaddy: *Does it matter?*

CurvyBabe: *It might.*

It doesn't. But in that same breath, it does, because I want to know more about this man who has me spilling my deepest desires and secrets tonight.

Silence stretches. Too long. I imagine him on the other side of the screen, weighing every word, or realizing I'm not worth the effort. The reality is, no matter how good he makes me feel, I still don't know who he is, and he's just some high-paying client.

But *he* knows me. Kind of. He knows what I wear, what I sound like when I come, what I hide behind the mask. He knows what I read, and my little confessions. That imbalance has always been there. I just didn't *feel* it until now.

Finally, the screen lights up again.

DineroDaddy: *Let's just say I'm closer than you think.*

My skin prickles. The hair on the back of my neck stands on end. Is this threatening or something else entirely?

CurvyBabe: *What's that supposed to mean?*

No reply.
Not right away.
My heart pounds, a mix of curiosity and something

darker threading through the cracks. I stare at the screen, waiting. Wanting. Dreading.

And then finally:

DineroDaddy: *You'll see. Soon.*

I don't know if it's a promise or a threat. I don't know if I should feel scared or not.

But I know this: I won't be sleeping tonight.

CHAPTER 5

THE NIGHT HE CRACKED

César

Like an office siren, she tempts me. I find myself walking by her office more times than I care to admit. Each time threatens to pull me under her spell, drown me in a desire so potent it's all consuming. I've had my fair share of women and felt lust before. All of it paled compared to this feeling now. Lety is the forbidden fruit I desperately want to taste for myself.

Today she's wearing a dress that hugs her curves sinfully, making my body heat with each roaming glance. Her long, brown legs are on full display as I walk by toward the end of the day under the guise of checking in on my employees. Truth be told, I don't notice or care about anyone else. I'm checking in on her. Lety's head is down as she reads something on her computer. Her beautiful brown eyes are hidden behind her thick, black lashes. She bites her bottom lip in concentration, and my cock stiffens at the sight of her.

The power this woman has over me...and she doesn't even know it.

She hasn't noticed I'm here, watching her like a fucking creep. I lean against the doorframe, expecting the groan of the wood to rouse her. It doesn't.

So, I watch. Like my own private showing. Only this time, she isn't CurvyBabe, and I'm not DineroDaddy. I'm her boss, and she's my employee. This is all kinds of fucked up and goes against HR policies I helped create. However, I can't bring myself to care. Rules were meant to be broken. And for the boss, some rules didn't apply. At least that's what I'm telling myself.

After a few moments of my girl being completely absorbed in whatever the fuck she's doing, I clear my throat from just outside her door.

Lety glances up—and jumps. Her eyes go wide, and she gasps, clutching her chest like her heart's about to give out. "Are you trying to kill me?" she hisses, voice sharp and breathless. It's her standard greeting to me when I sneak up on her.

I can't help the smirk that spreads across my face. She looks so thoroughly startled, it's almost impressive.

"Didn't think I was that scary," I tease, then chuckle when she glares at me. Anyone else would roll over and show me their bellies simply because I'm the boss. But Lety? Mi Reina? Nah, she shows her claws.

"Can I help you with something, Mr. Estrada?" She wields my last name like a weapon, pinning me with her stare. "If you put another file down on my desk, I may scream."

"If I was going to make you scream, Mrs. Zavala, it wouldn't be with a file." The words slip free before I can stop them, but once out, I find I don't regret them. Especially when I notice the adorable blush coloring her cheeks. I've successfully rendered her speechless and proven that she's not as unaffected by me as she pretends to be.

"How much more do you have to do?" I ask before she can respond.

Still in a daze and unsure about me, she shrugs. "Probably a few hours more."

"Give it to Melanie. You're coming with me."

"I'm what?" She sputters indignantly. "Unless you want me to have to redo everything Melanie touches, you best let me finish my work."

I ignore her and step into her office without so much as a word. The air between us thickens, the temperature seeming to rise the moment I cross the threshold. Lety stiffens, clearly not thrilled by the intrusion, but I don't give her a chance to object.

Without acknowledging the sharp look she throws my way, I lean in and press the lid of her laptop closed with a quiet finality. "We're leaving in ten minutes."

"César, I can't just—"

"I'll meet you out front. My car." I cut her off just as her voice bubbles with frustration, already turning away.

Behind me, I hear her sputter in disbelief, but I don't stop. I walk out, leaving her to stew in her irritation. I'm a fucked-up man because it makes me smile. I also know she'll follow me, wondering what the hell I'm up to.

❧ · ❧ · ❧ · ❧

"ARE you going to tell me why you kidnapped me?" An irate Lety asks from the passenger's seat. She crosses her arms over her chest, which pushes her tits up in an almost obscene manner. If I were a better man, I'd avert my gaze. Except I'm very much not a better man, so I keep sneaking glances at my assistant. I've seen her bare tits before, but only through a screen.

"You willingly came into my car," I remind again, having just had this same discussion not five minutes ago.

"Is that what you'll tell the cops when they find my dead body in the dumpster behind the alley?" She glares.

I raise a brow, earning an embarrassed blush from her.

"Sorry. I've been watching a lot of *Dateline*," she admits. "And I'm tired and hungry, which isn't a good combination for me. We've worked together long enough for you to know that."

My lips twitch to a smile. "Then I'll feed you."

"You've been feeding me all week, César. I appreciate it, but you don't have to continue to do that." She squirms in her seat, though I'm not sure if it's from nerves or something else.

"Let me take care of you," I murmur, turning down my street and easing the car past the wrought iron gates of my neighborhood. The community is exclusive, lined with sprawling estates. Each one is unique in architecture, but all boast the same air of wealth and grandeur. Manicured lawns. Stone facades. Homes that whisper old money and power.

From the corner of my eye, I see Lety relax her shoulders, looking more at ease in my car. "Fine, but can we do Chinese this time? Don't get me wrong, those street tacos have been delicious, but I'm ready for some shrimp fried rice."

I would buy her the whole damn restaurant if she wanted it. Except I think that would overwhelm her, and that's the opposite of what I want to do. So, I nod. "Shrimp fried rice it is. As long as we can get wonton soup with it."

"That's a given."

Her bratty response makes the corner of my mouth quirk up.

I'm keenly aware that I don't bring women home. Ever. My house is off-limits—a personal sanctuary where the line between business and pleasure stays clear. But Lety... Lety isn't just anyone.

She's different.

She's *mine*—or she will be, if I can manage not to fuck this up. But I'm done being patient. I'm a viper, ready to sink my fangs into her.

I've never been the type to settle down. Never saw the appeal. Women have always been a temporary indulgence. Lety, though? She consumes me. Takes up all my waking thoughts. I think about her constantly—her sharp tongue, the way her eyes flash when she's annoyed, how her voice lowers when she's tired or vulnerable. She's in my head when I wake up and when I fall asleep. I catch myself watching her when she isn't looking, memorizing the curve of her neck, the way her fingers fly over the keyboard when she types. She makes me irrational, possessive.

No woman has ever occupied my thoughts the way she does. No one has ever made me want more. It's a new sensation, but it feels right. Like I was always meant to find my way to her. Now I just need to convince her of the same.

She's quiet as I pull into the driveway, and I don't blame her. The house is a lot. Floor-to-ceiling windows, clean modern lines, wide driveway, and manicured hedges. Lety's eyes widen as she takes it all in, but she doesn't say anything. She just tightens her arms over her chest and stares ahead.

"I don't usually bring people here," I tell her as I shut off the engine. "You're the first." And she will be the last, but telling her that might freak her out. I need my girl to get used to the thought of us. Because "us" is an inevitability.

She arches a brow. "Should I feel honored or concerned?"

"Honored." I give her a crooked smile. "But if it makes you feel better, I'll let you keep your phone in case you want to call *Dateline* to report me yourself."

It's meant to be a joke, and luckily it lands. Lety lets out a small, reluctant laugh, but it's a win. She follows me out of the car and up the steps, her heels clicking lightly on the stone. I unlock the door and push it open, gesturing for her to enter.

The lights come on with a soft hum, casting a warm glow across the open floor plan. My place is clean thanks to the fantastic cleaning service I hired. The room is decorated in tasteful furniture in neutral tones that complement the dark wood floors and abstract art I didn't choose but paid way too much for. I watch her take it all in, fingers twitching at her sides like she's resisting the urge to touch something.

"You live here alone?" she murmurs, almost accusatory. Like any minute a wife and a kid I've never told her about will walk out and catch us.

"I do." I set my keys in a glass bowl near the door and turn back to her. I'm not surprised she asks because the house could fit two families comfortably.

She doesn't say anything as I lead her farther into the house, but I can feel the tension radiating off her in waves.

She's not used to this—being taken care of without having to ask. She's used to men watching her and wanting her body, but never *her*. Not really. That's what I gathered from our private chat as DineroDaddy and CurvyBabe.

"Make yourself comfortable," I say, gesturing to the plush seating area sunk into the floor just past the kitchen. She hesitates, but it's fleeting, because she soon kicks off her heels, letting out a content sigh.

"You're so lucky you don't have to wear heels," she murmurs under her breath.

With more confidence than before, Lety keeps her head up as she moves to sit on the couch. She sinks into the soft cushion, making herself comfortable. Most of her earlier nerves have gone away, as her body relaxes, looking more at home here. I can't help but wonder what it would feel like to lay her out and feast upon her until she begs me to stop. The thought hardens my cock, and I clear my throat, needing to look away. I want to seduce her, not scare her with a raging hard on. At least, not yet.

Except I can't help but notice how well she belongs in my home—like a permanent fixture that was always meant to be here. She makes herself cozy on my couch, tucking her feet under her as she reaches for a throw pillow to put behind her head. She must sense me staring at her because she looks up, raising an annoyed brow. "Well? Are you going to order food?"

I laugh and disappear to grab the wine I'd left chilling this morning. I dig my phone out of my pocket and locate the closest Chinese restaurant that delivers. By the time I return, food has been ordered, but before I can let her know, she startles like she forgot I was here. Or maybe she just forgot she was alone with me. In my home.

I pour the wine, offering her a glass. She takes it from

me with a small "Thanks," before bringing it up to her lips. I take the opportunity to sit close to her on the couch. I do it deliberately, feeling the heat of her body, but make sure to keep a little distance between us to ease her nerves. Lety readjusts herself, causing her to scoot closer to me on her own accord. Our legs touch, and if she notices, she doesn't pull away. I test the waters and angle my body closer, allowing more of our thighs to touch.

"You always *this nice* with your employees?" she asks, arching a brow. The way she says "nice" makes it sound like something more.

"Only the ones I can't stop thinking about." I sip my wine; my eyes locked on her lips. My filter is gone. I'm done toying around her, needing her to know who I really am. Not just her boss. And now that I have her alone, lured her here under the guise of work, I don't plan on holding back any longer. "And don't pretend you don't like the attention."

She scoffs, cheeks flushing. "You don't know what I like."

"Oh, *I do*." My voice dips low, and I watch the way her throat works as she swallows. A red flush creeps across her cheeks as her fingers flex around the wineglass. She doesn't move away. That's important. That's not to say she isn't warring with herself—that she's not fighting her desires.

But she's also not leaving.

"You've been feeding me, complimenting me, dragging me into your car like a damn caveman. What's this, César? Are you trying to wear me down until I fold? Is that your sick way of hazing me?" Her voice cuts deep, both anger and something that sounds a lot like fear mingling.

Fear that if she opens herself up to the idea of me that she won't be able to close me out again, perhaps?

"No." I lean in slightly, letting my voice fall soft. "I'm trying to get you to stop pretending you don't want this, too. That you don't want me."

She laughs, sharp and forced. Her thighs squeeze together, giving away her desire for me. "You're my boss. You sign my checks. There *is* no 'this.'" She gestures between us.

I tilt my head, studying her. "And if I wasn't your boss? If I was just some guy you met at a bar? Or online? What then? It wouldn't matter, would it?" I ache to tell her I know her. Who she really is. I don't want to be her fucking boss right now. I want to be *hers*.

"Maybe not to you, but I've worked too hard to be seen as more than a body. I'm not some assistant you get to play with until you're bored."

I set down my wine and shift closer, close enough that my knee brushes against hers. She thinks I want to play with her? To discard her once I'm done to chase after the next shiny thing that runs my way in heels? I've never given her a reason to think otherwise, but that stops now.

"Good," I say, voice low and deliberate. "Because I'm not bored. And I've never been one to play when it comes to you." She needs to know this isn't another fling. That her hold on me is unmatched.

The things I would do to please this woman...

She stills, hands clutching her wineglass so hard her knuckles turn white. I'm surprised she hasn't shattered it, and I'm pissed that she still doesn't understand I'm not playing. But maybe words aren't enough for her. A girl like Lety needs to see and feel the words in action. And I've been proving my loyalty for her a lot longer than either of us realize. On DesireDen.

"I see the way you look at me when you think I'm not

watching," I continue. "The way you lean into my touch whenever I brush too close. The way your eyes drop to my mouth when you're mad at me. I think you want me, Lety. Just like I want you. You're just too afraid to admit it. Maybe because you don't think I want you. Even though I've stayed with you in the office every night. Wanting to be near you. Wanting to talk to you. Wanting to make sure you're safe."

Her lips part, but no sound comes out. I reach out and drag a knuckle down the length of her jaw. She shivers.

"I've never been obsessed with a woman before," I admit. "But you?" I chuckle humorlessly, unable to stop the shiver racing up my spine. "You crawl under my skin. You haunt me. You think I'm being generous because I like to feed you? I'm *starving*, Lety. For you."

Her breath catches.

I lean in until my lips hover just over her ear. I hammer in the final nails in the coffin with just four little words.

"I *know* it's you."

Her whole body jolts, and I think she's about to make a run for it. But she doesn't. Instead, she sucks in a deep breath, waiting for me to confirm it.

"You're CurvyBabe."

She shoves back off the couch, eyes wide, as she tries to put distance between us. Now I've got her. My girl bares her teeth at me. "What the actual fuck?"

I rise slowly, giving her space to ease the confusion and horror I see on her face. When I speak, I try to keep my voice soft. Light. "I've known for a while now, mi reina. I've been watching you. Admittedly, I didn't know it was you at first. Not until I saw that pretty little butterfly tattoo on your back. But then it all made sense. Everything clicked for me. My draw to you—why you live rent free in my mind."

Her chest rises and falls, rapid and uneven. "How the hell—*why the hell*—César, that's private!"

"No, sweetheart," I murmur, taking another slow step forward, backing her into the wall behind her, "that's *intimate.* And I've been part of that world longer than you realize. So, I'm not leaving. Not unless you force me to."

Her jaw trembles, her panting breaths a mixture of fear and desire. "You're saying you've been...watching me?"

"I've done more than just watch." I smirk. "I've tipped. Subscribed. Favorited every goddamn video. I know what makes you squirm. I know what makes you moan. I've seen you come on your fingers, wishing it was my cock that made your scream like that. I've talked to you privately, listened to your secrets—and I never once shied away."

She stares at me, eyes wide and pupils dilated, horrified and aroused all at once.

"I'm your top supporter. Every night you were on, I was there. Every time you wore that little red lace number, you were thinking of your fans. But I was thinking of *you.*"

"You're insane," she breathes.

"Only about you, mi reina."

I close the last bit of distance between us. Her back hits the wall, and I press my hand beside her head, caging her in. She doesn't push me away. Doesn't scream.

Because part of her likes it.

The power. The heat. The obsession.

"You could fire me for this," she whispers.

"I won't," I promise. "But I'll fuck you for it."

She lets out a strangled sound, her eyes narrowing even as her thighs shift to press tightly together. I can see her resolve crumbling, breath by breath. I want to break down her barriers and strip her bare. I want to see every part of her she keeps locked away. I won't run from it. I'll fucking embrace it.

"You think I'm lying to you. That you're just another fleeting romance," I murmur, voice against her cheek. "But the truth is, you've been luring me in from the start. Every sigh. Every stretch. Every time you walked into my office like you didn't know exactly what that skirt was doing. I think you wore it just for me, didn't you?"

She shudders, and that's confirmation enough.

"Tell me to stop," I say.

She doesn't, only licks her lips and meets my eyes with a challenge in her gaze. Almost like she doesn't quite believe me.

So, I kiss her.

Hard.

Not soft or gentle or sweet because that's not what she needs. She's been screaming that into the void, and no one has noticed. Not until me. She needs the truth. The fire that's been eating us both alive.

My hand tangles in her hair, angling her mouth to take more. Her lips part with a needy sound, and I drink her in like I've been dying of thirst.

She kisses me back like she's finally letting herself break. Her hands fist my shirt, yanking me closer, dragging me down with her. A low groan leaves the back of my throat as my cock hardens painfully.

When I pull back, her lips are swollen. Her eyes are wild and glassy. She looks drunk. Drunk on me.

"I know it's you," I whisper again, reminding her as I brush my mouth along her jaw and throat. "And I don't want just *CurvyBabe*. I want *Lety*. I want both of you." She is the same person, but also different. I won't force her to choose one over the other. I'm a greedy bastard. I will take both.

"You're an asshole," she says, voice wrecked. Yet she doesn't pull away. Her body arches to me, as she traps my leg between her thighs.

"Say you want this." *Say you want me.*

"I don't want this." *Lie.* Almost a good one, if her voice hadn't come out breathy and her hand didn't trail over the hard muscles of my chest. Again, my cock twitches in interest, desperate to be buried deep inside of her.

For a moment, I have her. She's mine. Acceptance glows in her eyes.

But then something snaps in her. She dons a mask like she's been doing every damn day, putting up walls that had been so close to tumbling down mere moments ago. Her hand presses flat against my chest, using force to push me back. I stagger, but mostly out of confusion.

"I have to go."

"Lety—" I reach for her, but she dodges my grasp, grabbing her purse from the couch and putting it between us like a barrier.

"Let me go, César. *This*"—she gestures between us—"is too much. I need to go. Need to clear my head. You just dropped a fucking bombshell on me and expect me to just recover? Well, I can't. I need time to think. Let me go."

Every part of me wants to argue. To make her understand why this—us—is right. How could she not feel what is happening between us? Maybe she did and her first instinct is to run from it. But keeping her here will only hurt her, and that's the last fucking thing I want to do. So, for now, I have to let her go to win her heart.

"At least let me take you home."

But my girl is stubborn to the bone. She shakes her

head once adamantly. "I'll call an Uber. Goodbye, César." Her voice is tight, controlled in that way she gets when she's trying not to feel too much. Before I can get a single word out, she turns her back on me.

My hand twitches, half-lifting to stop her, but she's already moving to the door.

It all happens too fast.

One moment she's in front of me, eyes wide and mouth trembling with everything she won't say—and the next, she's gone. She flees for the door like it might save her from what just happened between us.

I don't react. Not right away. My brain lags, struggling to make sense of it. Did I say too much? Was it the truth that scared her, or the way I said it?

The door opens with a rush of cool night air.

She doesn't look back.

Just like that Lety slips through my fingers. Gone. And all I can do is stand there, surrounded by the lingering scent of her perfume and the aftertaste of a kiss that meant more to me than it ever should have.

I stare at the door long after it clicks shut.

I should go after her.

I *want* to go after her.

But I don't.

Because for the first time in a long time, I don't know how. But I make a silent vow to myself to give Lety the time to think. Because she will be mine.

CHAPTER 6

FLESH AND FIRE

Lety

I don't go back to work for a week. After I ran out of César's house upon the revelation of him being DineroDaddy, César texted to ask me if I made it home safe and he has called me three times. I didn't answer, but he could see I read the message. After the third day, I turned my phone off. I'm not certain if I fear he'll continue to call, or if I fear he won't. It's fucked up, but I blame him for these thoughts raging through my mind. He dropped a fucking bombshell on me, and now I'm left to pick up the fucking pieces.

César is DineroDaddy. He knows everything. Has seen *everything*. Being in this industry, I've always known that it was only a matter of time before someone from my personal life found out about my online presence. I just never expected it to be my boss. The man who can have any woman he wants. I've known men like him my whole life. Hell, I've dated men like him and suffered broken heart after broken heart because of them.

I can't have that again. I refuse.

And yet, my traitorous body longs to be close to César again. To be kissed like I'm his obsession and he can't get enough of me. Remembering the way my body was primed and heated for him—I had been so close to throwing my inhibitions out the window and letting my boss fuck me against the wall. Even thinking about his hands on me has my nipples hardening and clit begging to be touched.

The most shocking part of being at his house wasn't hearing him say he wanted to fuck me. Honestly, I'd half expected that after everything he said. But finding out he'd been watching me? That definitely rattled me—and maybe turned me on a little—then confused the hell out of me. But even that didn't compare to what really knocked the air from my lungs.

He didn't just want a night with me. He didn't just want my body.

He wanted *me*.

All of me. Every guarded piece I've never let anyone touch. No games. No walls. No camera. No pretending this was just some casual thing. He wanted something *real* —something raw. And I hadn't seen that coming. Not from him. He wasn't a relationship man, and I couldn't be a relationship woman. Things would get cloudy and messy too quickly.

I grab my full glass of chardonnay, taking a sip. I can't avoid him forever. Not unless I want to quit my job, and I don't. César said he wouldn't fire me, but I can't bank on that. I've had one too many vicious boyfriends that would do anything to get back on me. I don't think César would stoop to that level, but I've been burned in the past, and I'm not eager to relive that pain.

So, I need to make a decision, and fast.

Right after I finish a glass of chardonnay. Or two.

᷍ · ᷍ · ᷍ · ᷍

THE OFFICE IS UNUSUALLY hectic for a Friday. Normally, by this time, half the staff has already dipped out early, leaving the place quiet and half-empty. But today? Everyone's still here, and it's chaos. Phones are ringing nonstop, heels clack against the tile as people rush past, and the hum of overlapping conversations makes it hard to think straight.

Something feels off. The energy is frenzied, almost panicked, and I can't shake the sense that I walked into the middle of a storm no one warned me about.

I pass Melanie's desk and nearly roll my eyes. She's drowning in a mountain of paperwork, one hand gripping the phone, the other flipping through files like her life depends on it. She's flailing, barely keeping up, and I can't help but think it's karma for all the times she half-assed her job and left everyone else to pick up the slack so she could pretend to talk to her imaginary boyfriend. Maybe if she got it right the first time, she wouldn't be stuck trying to salvage the mess now.

I'm also a little too tipsy to be here, so confronting my boss at his place of work is probably a bad idea. Actually, it's a really fucking stupid idea. The wine sloshing around inside of me doesn't seem to care, though, and I'm already here.

"Oh, thank heavens, Lety, you're back!" Melanie disconnects her call, pushing out of her chair. She charges over to me like she's about to hug me, but we ain't cool like that, so I side-step her.

"Not for long. Where's César?" I ask, noticing a slight slur to my words.

Clearly Melanie does too and raises a razor-thin eyebrow. "You mean, Mr. Estrada? I assume he's in his office. I think he's in a meeting—Hey, wait! You shouldn't interrupt him!"

I leave Melanie standing alone at her desk, calling after me. The others in the office curiously glance up as I pass. This isn't like me. I don't make waves at work, and from my walk and speech, it's clear I've been a little too generous on the wine. I'll come to regret this later. Maybe. But right now, I have a one-track mind.

I stab the elevator button with my finger repeatedly until the doors finally open. I all but barrel past the people exiting before pressing César's floor. With excruciating slowness, the elevator doors close, and I ascend. This would be a good time for me to think of what exactly I'm going to say to César when I see him, but the ride is too short. Soon, the elevator dings and the doors open onto his floor.

It's quiet here, only the soft clacks of the keyboard and the urgent taps of my heels against the tile floor ring out. Gracie looks up from the computer as I pass her, but she's on the phone and only gives me a confused look. For now, I ignore it as I beeline for César's office. The door is closed, and I test the knob.

Not locked. Good.

I push the door open—with far more force than neces-sary—and it hits the wall with a loud bang. César's head shoots up, lips pursed as I barge in unceremoniously. "We need to talk." This time, I'm certain my words are slurred. I am also seeing double of him, which probably means I'm too drunk for this shit.

"I'll have to call you back," César says into the phone, pressing a button before ending the call. My cheeks flush at the realization he had been in the middle of a meeting. He continues to eye me, and I try not to wilt under his scrutiny. "Lety. I wasn't expecting you."

I wasn't expecting to be here, but since I am, I slam the door behind me, making sure it clicks shut before storming further into the room.

"You kissed me!" I blurt out, skipping any kind of greeting or buildup. No small talk, no warm-up. Just straight to the damn point. My voice echoes a little too loud, fueled by the wine still buzzing in my system. It's the only thing I can think to say—raw and unfiltered, the truth spilling out before I can second-guess it.

"I did." There's no emotion in his voice. Sterile. Giving nothing away.

"You said you wanted me."

"I did that, too, mi reina."

"Don't call me that," I snap, but my body betrays me, growing hot at the nickname. I like it too much to pretend I don't.

César notices. Of course this asshole does. His perfect lips snake up into a smirk as he pushes himself from his chair. He closes this distance between us in a few strides. I back up to try to put some distance between us, but my back connects to the wall. I'm back where this all started again, and he effectively cages me. His muscular body pins me in place, and every nerve on my body stands on end.

Fuck this man.

César leans down, and I'm consumed by the smell of him. "You've been ignoring me, Lety."

I open my mouth to deny it, but nothing comes out. He's right, and the bastard knows it.

"You leave for a week. Everyone showed their incompetence while you're gone. I don't pay you enough for what you do."

I scoff. "You really want to talk about my pay, now?" I pause before adding, "But you're right. I need a raise."

"Done." The word barely leaves his mouth before he leans in. He's nearly as close as he was that night at his house—too close, and yet not close enough.

His lips hover a breath away from mine, and my body leans toward him instinctively, pulled by something unseen, something undeniably him. A brujo spell. My lips tingle with anticipation, a phantom memory of how his kiss once felt—soft, demanding, unforgettable. I crave to experience that again.

"I don't know what to say to you." I'm regretting the second glass of chardonnay, unable to think clearly. That could also be with the close proximity of his body and the way I crave to feel his lips and hands on me. I'm a horny mess and had no business barging in under these circumstances.

"Then maybe we don't talk." César's gaze drops to my mouth. My tongue slips out to wet my suddenly dry lips, and something shifts in his eyes, darkening with heat. His hand lifts, fingers brushing my cheek before settling against the side of my face. His thumb grazes my bottom lip, slow and deliberate, like he's memorizing the shape of it.

"I haven't stopped thinking about that damn kiss," he murmurs, voice low and rough. "Not since the night you walked out and left me hard and alone."

My face heats. "You scared me, César."

"And you scared me, mi reina. I was fucking gutted when you walked out."

"You can't say things like that and expect me to be okay with it," I say weakly, still not able to comprehend why this man feels the need to want me when there's a whole line of women who would die to get into his bed and not be as difficult as I am. But maybe that's what he likes best? The chase.

"You allergic to the truth, mi reina?"

"I'm allergic to men."

"Nah, Lety. You're allergic to boys who try to be men—to those who can't appreciate the woman you are. I'm not that type of man and never will be."

"How do I know that?" My voice is so small, barely a whisper. My resolve is crumbling, and fast. I've been content being by myself. Living my life as a cam model and swearing off men. But loneliness still takes over in the middle of the night. The urge to wrap myself up in the arms of someone who sees me—*truly* sees me—is becoming nearly impossible to ignore. I've just never been able to pick out good men. I love too hard, and it all comes crashing down around me in the end.

"Call it intuition, Lety, but I know I can be the man for you. I just need you to tear down those fucking walls, mi reina, and let me in."

I want to. So badly, I want to. But I'm also not willing to change the important things in my life for a man. Not even this one. No matter how badly I crave him. "If you plan on fucking me and moving on, you can fuck all the way off."

"I plan on fucking you and keeping you."

"Is this going to get me fired?"

"I already told you it wouldn't. Even if this ends, I won't let you go unless you ask to be let go."

"Well, I'm not stopping my work. I fucking love being

a sex worker and it makes me feel empowered. If you can't handle that, then—"

"Lety." César brings his thumb back to my lips, effectively cutting me off. There's amusement glimmering in his eyes, and the sight makes me blush. "I never asked you to quit, and I never will. I fucking love watching you. And now I'll love knowing your audience can see but not touch you. That you may come on your fingers or toys on camera, but you are coming on my cock and screaming my name afterward."

Fuck, this man.

This perfect, sexy man. How do I say no to that? I can't.

"I don't know how to be a good girlfriend," I admit. I'm giving this man every out in the book, so he can't blame me if this goes up in flames.

"Fair. I don't know how to be a good boyfriend. We'll figure this shit out together." César braces his hands on either side of my face, taking a step closer until our bodies align and I feel every inch of him. His cock digs into my thigh, and despite myself, I moan.

"You're mine, Lety. And I'm about to stake claim to what's mine. This is *your* last out. You stay and I'm unleashing myself on you."

Oh, fuck. His words sober me, grounding me in the moment.

"Anyone could walk in," I remind him, but my brain screams for me to stop talking.

"I guess you better be quiet." César doesn't give me a chance to respond. In an instant, his lips are on mine. Hard. Rough. Punishing. He kisses me like he's drinking me in and punishing me for leaving him the other night.

My body reacts to his, arching into him. I grind against

his thigh, desperate for some friction. His hand tangles in my hair, grabbing it in his fist and pulling. Pain and pleasure explode, and I let out a breathy moan.

The bastard chuckles.

"I'm not letting you get away from me this time, Lety," he growls against my lips.

I open my mouth to...argue? Agree? I don't know. I don't get the chance, though, because in the next moment his tongue is in my mouth, claiming and possessing.

I'm a woman undone.

César's arms come around my body, and with ease I didn't know was possible, picks me up. I'm not a skinny girl. I have a round, soft stomach. Thick thighs. Curves and rolls. I've never been picked up and carried across a room before, but César makes it seem easy. His muscles don't even look like they strain as he carries me.

I think I've officially met my match. That both terrifies and thrills me.

César sets me on his desk and moves between my legs. "I watch you play with that pretty pussy weekly. Watching you pump your fingers inside of you and tease that little clit. It's my turn," he growls.

"Yes, sir," I purr, earning a growl from him. He likes it. Good.

"Open your legs."

I do, or as much as I can in my skirt. The material bunches up, allowing me to part my thighs. But apparently, it's not good enough for César because he pushes my skirt up, spreading my legs wide and exposing my thong.

"Already wet for me."

That's an understatement. I'm drenched for him.

And then César, my boss, lowers himself to his knees. The image of this mighty billionaire lawyer on his knees for me will forever be ingrained in my head. I feel power-ful, sexy, and desired, something I've rarely felt with previous men.

César will be my undoing.

He braces his hands on my thighs, keeping me spread as if I would suddenly close my legs and change my mind. I won't. I'm far too gone for that. He leans in closer, his nose swiping along the apex of my thighs. I shudder, and I think he does, too.

César inhales a deep breath. "Fucking perfect," he murmurs.

Trailing his hands up my thighs, he hooks his thumbs through the top of my thong, tugging it down. I have to wiggle and help him get them off, but soon, they are around my ankles. I expect him to toss it to the floor, but instead, he folds them and places them in his suit pocket. I raise my brow, but he only smirks. "These are mine now."

Okay, then.

"You don't know how badly I've wanted to taste you, Lety. How much you've tormented me..."

A shudder sends warmth through my body. "Then do it."

César wastes no time. Like a viper, he strikes. His mouth finds my core, licking me from front to back.

"César!" I gasp, and all concept of being quiet thrown out the window.

This man takes no mercy on me, and I wouldn't have it if he did. He finds my clit, taking the sensitive bundle of nerves into his mouth. Fingers notch at my entrance before I feel the pressure of two of them pushing inside of me.

It's a lot. All at once.

And yet I crave more. He's made me a wanton woman

with nothing other than his tongue and two fingers. No man should harbor this much power.

César devours me with intent—every flick of his tongue, every curl of his fingers inside me is deliberate, practiced, and sexy. He's not just going down on me—he's unraveling me. This is a goddamned spiritual awakening.

My hips writhe beneath his mouth, chasing every pulse of pleasure he drags out of me with maddening precision. I reach down, desperate to touch him, and thread my fingers through his hair. It's silky and thick, soft enough that I know I'll crave the feel of it against my palms later—alone in bed, aching, remembering the way he made me fall apart with nothing but his mouth and that sinful determination.

And just like that, a future with César forms in my mind. It's tentative and fragile, but it's there. A possibility of what could happen if I allow it.

I ride my boss's face with wild abandon, chasing a high I haven't felt in a long time. He lets me use him for my pleasure, speeding up his fingers and sucking my clit harder, like he was born for this moment. Maybe he was. Maybe we both were.

Stars explode behind my vision, and I moan out his name. "César!" I chant his name with reverence as my orgasm rips through me, breaking me apart and putting me together again.

I fear I may never be satisfied by another man. Only him.

César pulls back slowly, his mouth wet, lips glistening with my release. He licks them with lazy satisfaction, a cocky smirk tugging at the corner of his mouth, like he knows exactly what kind of mess he's made of me.

"You're mine, Lety," he murmurs, voice rough with

possession. "And I'm not going to let you hide from me anymore."

The words sink into me deeper than his kisses ever could.

"I won't," I whisper, my voice still ragged from pleasure. It's a promise. A hopeful one. A scared one. One I pray I'm strong enough to keep.

My body is boneless, sprawled across his desk. My skin hums, over-sensitive and sated, every inch of me marked by his mouth, his hands, and his hunger. My breath stutters in and out as I blink up at the ceiling, still trying to catch up with what just happened.

Because this wasn't just him eating my pussy. It wasn't even just pleasure.

It was a claiming.

And for the first time, I don't want to run.

CHAPTER 7

TOO GOOD TO BE TRUE

Lety

I'm dating my boss. Me, the woman who swore off all men, is dating the man who signs my checks. I haven't decided if I'm the luckiest or dumbest woman alive. I'm still uncertain if this is a good idea, or if this is a dream I'll be waking up from soon enough. Either way, I can't regret my decision to stop running from César and let him pursue me.

When I left his office that evening he ravished my pussy, I expected eyes on me. Surely my face and slightly wrinkled clothing were a dead giveaway I had the boss on his knees. Except, no one paid me any attention. Not even when César walked me out to my car, walking far closer than appropriate, and kissed me in the middle of the parking garage.

Since then, I can't quite shake the tension in my body, like I'm waiting for the second shoe to drop.

It's been three days since our tryst in his office—and over a week since I've been back to work. He asked to take me out over the weekend, but I needed time alone to truly sober up and make sure I'm not making the biggest mistake of my life. I'm so damn tired of being lonely, and César seems like he truly wants this. Wants me. I would be foolish not to give us a shot, right?

I tell myself I'm ready to fall back into my usual routine, to find comfort in the rhythm of the workday. But the truth is, my nerves are shot to hell. My stomach flips with every step closer to the building, and anticipation is wound tight in my chest like a coil ready to snap.

I feel like a teenager sneaking around with the older boy her parents warned her about—thrilled by the danger but constantly glancing over her shoulder. The memory of his mouth on my skin, the way he said my name like it belonged to him, is still fresh and electric in my mind. It's exhilarating...and terrifying. I'm walking a fine line between excitement and anxiety, and my body doesn't know how to respond.

I'm nearly at the front entrance to the office, an hour early to work, when something darkens the entrance and I feel a presence behind me. A moment later, two muscular arms wrap around my center, pulling me back against a firm, hard body. My body relaxes against his, knowing it's César before he speaks.

"Good morning, Ms. Zavala." His lips brush against my neck, placing soft kisses that send a shiver racing down my spine.

"Morning, Mr. Estrada. Has anyone told you it's highly inappropriate to sneak up and kiss your employees?"

He chuckles, his breath tickling my neck. "I assure you, mi reina, my thoughts are much more inappropriate than my actions."

My body heats in response and wetness pools between

my thighs. "Oh?" I manage to squeak out, too turned on to be embarrassed by my breathy tone.

"Mm-hmm. Come with me," he murmurs and wraps his hand around my wrist, gently tugging me. "Work can wait."

"Yes, sir," I murmur. I half expect him to take me to his office, but he leads me back to the parking garage. "Where are you taking me?"

"Do you not like surprises?" He smirks, leading me toward a large, black Ford. The truck towers over the other cars in the garage by several feet. César touches the door handle and there's an audible click. The headlights flicker, and he opens the back door. "Get that pretty ass back there."

"You didn't answer my question." Even as I say it, I find myself crawling into the back seat of his truck. The air is still cool from the AC, not having warmed up in the unusually warm morning air.

"No, I didn't," is all he says. He doesn't move until I climb into the truck, and only then does he follow, sliding into the seat beside me. The doors shut with a heavy *thunk*, and the dark tint of the windows turns the space into a private cocoon that shields us from curious eyes and the world outside.

He turns to me, gaze steady, as he says, "I'm not taking you anywhere." The finality in his tone hangs between us like a closed door.

"Then what—"

He kisses me. He has a habit of cutting off my questions with panty-soaking kisses and I can't bring myself to be mad about it. His hand moves to cup my jaw, while the other tangles in my hair, pulling my head back just enough that I have no choice but to submit to his will.

"It's going to be torture working next to you all day and not being able to touch you," he growls against me. "So, I'm indulging now. I'm burying my cock into that sweet pussy, savoring every fucking second of it, mi reina. Going to fill you with my cum, so you'll feel me inside of you all day."

"Fuck, yes. César, I need you." I claw at his clothes with ravenous intent, wanting them gone.

His cocky laugh makes me snarl. "So fucking needy, Lety."

"Shut up."

This time, I'm the one who kisses him. It's rough, furious, and starved, like I haven't kissed him in years. There's no softness, no hesitation. Just teeth, tongue, and frustration. It's because I am angry—angry that he makes me feel this wild, desperate, and out of control. No man should have that much power over me, yet César does.

My hands go straight for his pants, fingers fumbling with the zipper like I've lost all patience. When I brush over the hard line of his dick, he groans. The sound is deep and guttural, like it is being ripped from his throat, is toe-curling.

It unleashes something in both of us.

Our bodies and hands are a whirlwind as we rip off clothes. César yanks my skirt down and cusses. I smirk, knowing he sees I've decided against panties today. "You're fucking sinful, Lety."

"I know." I didn't know that this would happen, but as I was getting ready this morning, part of me hoped for something to happen. I was going to be prepared, and clearly, it worked out.

I finally undo his pants, and I waste no time reaching

in, feeling his silk boxers before my hand wraps around a large cock.

"Fuck, César." I've had my fair share of dicks, and I've enjoyed them at any size, but something tells me that not only does he have a large cock, but he knows how to use it.

"Lay down."

His back seat is wide and comfortable. I lay back on the seat, spreading my legs wide. One look at the intensity swarming in his eyes tells me my core glistens with arousal. "Are you going to fuck me raw, sir?"

Again, he curses. It takes a moment for him to compose himself and I can't help the accomplished smirk that crosses my lips. "Can I?" Despite the heated moment, he still takes time to check in with me.

"Yes. I'm on birth control."

Thank God for birth control and regular STD screenings.

A smirk tugs at the corner of his lips. "Then yes, Lety. I'm fucking this pussy raw. It's mine."

"Then fucking do it."

His nostrils flare—and then he's on me again, crashing his mouth against mine in a kiss that's all hunger and heat.

His rough and greedy hands find my breasts, squeezing and rolling my nipples between his fingers until I gasp into his mouth. I writhe beneath him, hips shifting in search of relief, but he's got me pinned—his thighs bracketing mine, his grip holding me exactly where he wants me. Helpless, aching, and completely at his mercy.

Then I feel his heavy cock bob between us. I spare a glance down, seeing his erection. Just as I suspected, he's long and thick. His cock is slightly curved with a mushroom tip. I desperately want to take down my throat.

Soon. First, I need him inside of me. I *need* to feel the burn of the stretch and the feeling of being stuffed.

"Fuck. Me," I growl again. I run my nails down his back, earning a hiss from him.

"So fucking dirty. Are you my little slut, Lety?"

"Fuck..." I moan, nodding. I'll be whatever the fuck he wants me to be, as long as I feel his dick inside me.

"This what you want, mi reina?" He fists his cock and strokes himself. I whine underneath him, growing more frustrated by the moment.

"Either fuck me or I'll find someone who will." My words have the desired effect. His eyes narrow, darkening. He bares his teeth at me, and I know I'm in trouble.

"You can show this pretty pussy to the world, Lety. You can fuck it and come on camera. But I'm the only cock allowed inside it." His words make me tremble, but I don't get a chance to respond. He's notched at my entrance, and in one powerful thrust, he's sheathed balls-deep inside of me.

I scream.

He moans.

It's fucking bliss.

My walls tighten around him, screaming at how full he makes me feel. I wrap my legs around him, heels digging into the top of his ass.

"So fucking perfect," he moans into my ear. I arch my back, needing to feel more of him. It's both too much and not enough. My mind can barely comprehend the pleasure, even as it begs for more.

The truck rocks gently at first, the suspension squeaking beneath us with each movement, but it doesn't stay gentle for long. The scent inside is thick—leather seats warmed by the sun, a faint trace of his cologne, and now, the unmistakable musk of sex and sweat clinging to the air.

He thrusts into me without warning. Hard. Fast. Deep. His cock curves just right, dragging against my walls and hitting a spot so sensitive it sends sparks down my spine.

I cry out, the raw sound tearing from my throat without permission. It's not just pleasure—it's shock and need from the overwhelming stretch of him filling me completely.

The force of his rhythm builds, powerful and relentless. Each thrust slams into me with enough strength to make the whole truck lurch, the shocks creaking in protest. The windows may be tinted, but it hardly matters anymore. Anyone walking by could tell what's happening by the way the vehicle bounces, by the fogging glass and the rhythmic thud of bodies colliding.

His breath is sharp against my neck; the low growls escaping his throat vibrate against my skin. My hands scramble for purchase, digging into the seat, into his shoulders, trying to anchor myself against the onslaught of pleasure. But there's no control. No slowing down. Just the raw, desperate pace of him claiming me completely.

My walls tighten around him. His body shakes, shoulders tensing, and I know he's as close as I am. I open my mouth, but all that comes out is a moan. César reaches between us, thumb finding my clit and rubbing in slow, circular motions.

Pleasure erupts, and I scream. His moans mix with mine and soon we fall over the edge together. I come hard, just as his hot release fills me. He comes as if he hasn't finished in months. But so do I, feeling lightheaded when the high fades. My body is a mess of sweat and cum, but I fucking love it.

I'm marked by him.

"Such a good girl, Lety. Taking my cock like that," he groans into my ear, nipping at my lobe. Even that part of my body is sensitive.

César is slow to pull away, almost reluctant. The moment he pulls out of me, I feel empty. His release drips down my thighs, coating me even more. Before he can pull away any further, my hand snaps out and closes around his wrist. "Take...a picture...of me," I pant.

At first, he doesn't move, just raises an eyebrow, a silent question on his lips.

"I want to post a picture on my DesireDen."

He goes still at my explanation, every muscle tensing—and my heart sinks. For a breathless moment, I'm certain I've ruined everything. The air shifts, heavy with the weight of unspoken judgment.

Of course he wouldn't want me. No man ever truly does once they know what I've done—what I am. A small, bitter part of me whispers *"You should've known better."* I can already feel the walls rising, piece by piece, the armor I've spent years perfecting rebuilding itself to shield me from the pain I know is coming.

But then he grins. Not cruel. Not mocking. Just soft and knowing, like he sees every shattered part of me and still wants to stay.

"That's a fucking sexy idea," he says, reaching down on the floor for his pants. He pulls out his phone, aiming its camera at me. "Fuck, Lety, you look so good."

He begins snapping photos of me. I've never let anyone help me with my DesireDen account. This seems far more intimate than what we just did, but I can't deny the feeling of liking that he's not only willing to help but seems excited about it.

Is this man even real? I hate the doubt creeping in, he almost seems too good to be true. I try to keep it at bay for now.

Once he's done, César hands me back the phone. "Text the ones you like to your phone," he says, nuzzling my neck.

I can't help the smile on my face.

We lay there in comfortable silence; him softly kissing me while I look through the phone. After a few moments, he breaks the silence. "Lety?"

"Hmm?"

"Come with me to a party this weekend."

I pause, putting the phone down to get a better look at him. "A party?"

He nods. "As my date."

I flush at the word, even though we are so far beyond that. "What kind of party?"

"Just something small. I want to introduce you to a few people." He doesn't elaborate on who.

The old me wants to say no, to claim I'm busy, I have other plans, that this—*we*—is too complicated. It would be easier to protect myself before anything has the chance to hurt.

But if I keep saying no out of fear, I'll never know what we could be. And something about César—beyond the way he looks at me like I matter—makes me want to try.

"What should I wear?" I ask, my voice quieter than I intend.

"Whatever you want," he tells me, that confident glint in his eyes. "Just come."

A grin tugs at my lips. "I think we already did that."

He chuckles and leans in to kiss me. It's not rushed or hungry this time, but rather tender. A kiss that speaks of more than lust. A kiss that says *stay*. That says *trust me*.

"Come with me," he murmurs again, resting his forehead against mine.

My heart stutters. Fear lingers, but so does something else. Something like hope.

So, I nod. "Okay."

And as he pulls away, that hope blooms, fragile and real.

I just pray that glimmer of hope doesn't steer me wrong.

CHAPTER 8

FIESTA WITH A
SIDE OF DOUBT

Lety

What did one wear on a first date with their new boyfriend, who also happens to be your boss? What straddled the line between sexy and professionalism? It would have helped if César had given me more information about the party, but the most I got out of him was "look nice."

The fuck does that mean?

Luckily, I didn't end up having to figure out his words because a large, white box showed up to my door with a red bow on it and a card sticking out. I quickly grabbed the card and read the note.

Wear this tomorrow —César

The man bought me a dress. In my size. How the fuck he knew my size is beyond me, and I don't know if I'm flattered or concerned he knows these intimate details about me, but I'm too in love with the dress to care.

The day of the party, I slip on my new red dress, embracing the perfect balance between elegance and danger. Red is also my color, which César clearly picked up on. The fabric clings to my bodice, sculpting my figure with a deep neckline that toes the line between tasteful and sinful. The waist cinches just right before the skirt flares out in soft folds, brushing just below my knees. A subtle slit teases a glimpse of leg with every step, drawing the eye down to the strappy black heels I've been dying to wear—sexy, sharp, and long overdue for their moment.

The way César's eyes darken, the predatory look on his face when he picks me up, is a look I'll never forget.

"You picked out a good one," I say when he doesn't speak, too preoccupied with looking me over. "How did you know my size?"

"Guessed," he grunts, like a caveman only capable of single words. Then he says, "You look fucking breathtaking." His body—and truthfully, mine too—scream bedroom, and as much as I want to give into that temptation, I also don't want to ruin hours of hard work I spent to get ready to meet his friends.

Which is why I lead us to his, making sure we are both buckled in and ready for whatever the hell he has planned for us.

"Are you going to tell me where we're going, or do you just like keeping me in the dark?" I ask when I can no longer stand the silence between us.

César's lips quirk up in a half smile. "You don't trust me?"

"It has nothing to do with trust, and everything to do with being a nosey bitch and wanting to know where my boy—" I cut myself off. Calling him my boyfriend still feels so strange on my tongue. Not bad, exactly, just different. Different can be good, right? There's no doubt I like him

—crave him even—but there's still a part of me that doesn't believe I deserve him.

César's grip on the steering wheel turns his knuckles white. His big truck suddenly feels like a clown call.

"I'm not your boyfriend, Lety."

His words slice through me, sharper than any blade. The air leaves my lungs in a staggered gasp as if he's just struck me in the chest. My vision blurs with tears that threaten to spill before I can blink them away. A tremble runs through my hands.

How could he say that after everything? After the way he looked at me, touched me, whispered things no one else ever had? I thought I meant something more. I *felt* it. God, had I imagined all of it?

My heart twists painfully in my chest, each beat hammering the same cruel question: Did I get it all wrong?

Maybe he does want me—but not in the way I'd hoped. Not in the way I need.

Before I can go further down this dark path, César takes my face in his hands. I try to flinch away, but he holds me in place. I didn't even notice he stopped driving and had pulled up to a fancy-looking hotel, too consumed with my own spiraling thoughts after his shitty words.

"I'm not your boyfriend, Lety."

Is this man fucking serious? Now I'm pissed. "I heard you the first fucking time, you dick. I'm just another mark in your bed, is that it? You know, you really had me believing I was worth something to you." I let out a bitter laugh, holding back a sob. "I can't believe—"

"I'm not your boyfriend, Lety, because what I feel for you can't be captured with such a pathetic title."

My breath hitches in my throat for a completely different reason.

"What do you mean?" I all but whisper, not wanting to get my hopes up.

"I mean that you're my future. You've taken over every part of me—my thoughts, my breath, even the space in my chest where my heart once lived. 'Boyfriend'?" He shakes his head, eyes burning into mine. "That word feels too small. Too temporary. Like something high school kids whisper in hallways. What I feel for you is deeper. It's permanent. It's *real.* So no, I'm not your boyfriend. I'm your man. And you're my queen. Do you understand me?"

My heart pounds rapidly in my chest. A feeling blossoms low in my belly. It's bright. Airy. And completely terrifying. I can do little more than nod. It seems to satisfy him.

"Good girl," he murmurs, and leans in to kiss me. It's just a faint touch of his lips. There and gone in seconds. "Now, get that sexy ass out of my truck so I can show you off."

♥ · ♥ · ♥ · ♥

THE HOTEL DOUBLES as an event center, often rented out by companies and people with more money than they know what to do with. We're directed to a room on the first floor, one already humming with conversation and clinking glasses.

Floor-to-ceiling windows stretch along one side, offering a view of the landscaped outdoor amenities and swaying trees. Inside, round tables draped in crisp white linens are arranged throughout the space, each adorned with elegant floral centerpieces. Along one wall, a group of waiters busily prepare trays of food, while others glide through the crowd to offer drinks. Crystal chandeliers hang overhead, scattering soft, rainbow-like light across the polished floor. Classical music plays from somewhere in the room.

"What kind of party is this?" I ask once we're inside. A server carrying glasses of what I hope is wine comes by and offers me one, which I take. César takes one, too, but doesn't seem impressed by it as he scans the crowd.

"A celebratory party for one of my old friends. He just opened this hotel less than a month ago. Now he's ready to show it off," he answers before taking a sip of the wine. He makes a sour face, placing the glass down on an empty table.

"I'll take that," I say and scoop it up. Double-fisting two glasses of wine is pretty on-brand for me. But for ease, I pour the rest of his drink into mine before taking a sip. "It's not bad."

"It's also not great."

He has a point there, but wine is wine. I've survived off worse.

César places a hand on my back, guiding me deeper into the room. As I glance around at the guests, I'm relieved to see that my outfit fits right in. César is dressed in a black suit, expertly tailored to his frame. His crisp white shirt is unbuttoned at the top, revealing just a hint of the sculpted chest I know lies beneath. The other men wear suits, too, but César doesn't just wear his. He owns it.

"Are you hungry?" he asks me, head swiveling around the room as if he's looking for someone.

Before I can answer, a deep, masculine voice comes from behind us. "César, who let your ugly ass in?"

I turn just in time to see a man approaching us. He's tall—easily César's height—with a powerful build that fills out his tailored black suit. The fabric clings to his arms and shoulders, emphasizing a broad chest and the kind of physique that suggests both discipline and strength. His beard is neatly trimmed, framing a sharp jawline, and his jet-black hair is cropped short, every strand perfectly in place. There's an effortless elegance about him, like he could've just stepped off a runway or out of a high-end fashion spread.

He's not alone, though. A beautiful and petite woman hangs on his arm, and although she's smiling—her pretty red lips the same shade as my own—it doesn't meet her eyes. The way the two of them walk together is also awkward, more like they are putting on a show rather than a real couple.

César drops his hand from my back, going over to give the stranger one of those weird hugs men give where they slap each other's back and squeeze their hand in a death grip. "I know damn well you ain't calling me ugly, fool."

Neither of these men are ugly. Not even close. Even the way they laugh is handsome.

The two break away, and the man's gaze falls to me, quickly sweeping over my body before backing up. His face is unreadable, schooled like a politician, and yet somehow kind. "And what poor woman did you force to accompany you?"

The wine encourages me to move forward and offer my hand. "I'm Lety Zavala. I came here willingly, don't worry."

The man laughs and extends his large hand to take mine, gently shaking it. "Thank you for coming, Ms. Zavala. Even if you have the misfortune of coming with César."

The man in question rolls his eyes before wrapping his arm around me, pulling me back to the side. I can't help but notice the side eye the woman gives me as she takes in the two of us. I do my best to ignore it for now.

"Lety, this is Augustín Cisneros and his wife, Carmen," César introduces.

"We've never seen you before," Carmen says by way of greeting. "How did the two of you meet?" Innocent enough question, but it feels loaded coming from her.

I also don't know how to answer. It's not exactly taboo that I'm dating my boss, but it's not entirely proper, either. We should have discussed this first, and I'm mentally kicking myself for not thinking about this sooner.

"Lety and I have worked together for a while now," César says, voice confident, with none of the hesitation tightening my chest.

Carmen hums, arching one perfectly drawn brow. She taps her manicured nail against the rim of her champagne glass. "Workplace romance. Bold."

Her words aren't rude, but something about her tone cuts deeper than I expect. Is this going to be the normal reaction when people hear about César and me? If so, I better get used to it. I manage a small smile and glance away, sipping the wine that suddenly tastes a little sour.

César doesn't seem fazed. "Bold is one word. I call it inevitable."

Carmen laughs lightly, one hand still resting on Augustín's arm. Her eyes never leave mine, though. "I suppose it depends on the kind of woman. Not everyone can handle what comes with a man like César. He's definitely had his fair share of dates."

I can't tell if it's a warning or a compliment. Maybe

both. I know for certain I don't like her. How can one person look both bored and disgusted at the same time?

Before I can decide how to respond, Augustín gestures toward a group of sharply dressed men gathering near the back of the room. "Come, hermano. I want to introduce you to a few of the investors I was telling you about."

César turns to me. "You'll be okay for a bit?"

I nod quickly, because what other choice do I have? Tell him not to go because I don't want to be alone with Carmen? Fuck that. "Of course."

He leans in, brushing his lips against my cheek in a move that's equal parts possessive and intimate. "I won't be long."

God, I hope he's not.

Then the men head off, leaving me standing with Carmen, who lets out a long sigh the moment they're out of earshot. I don't miss the glare she gives her husband as he walks away.

Interesting.

"Men," she says, like it's the ultimate curse word. And yeah, I get it. We can agree on that at least. "They love talking numbers and pretending the world can be bought and sold with charm and ego."

I offer a polite smile, unsure what to say.

She studies me for a beat. "You're beautiful," she says finally, almost like she's disappointed that I am. "That dress is perfection on you. César has good taste."

"Thank you," I offer, a little thrown off by the unexpected compliment.

"I mean it. It's no small thing, showing up to a place like this with men like them. The women here can be just as cutthroat. From how many women César has dated, I worried he'd never meet his match. But maybe you're the exception."

I bristle but try to keep my face neutral. I know she's looking for a reaction, and I'm not going to give her that if I can help it.

"I noticed," I murmur, trying to sound disinterested while I'm fuming inside. Because who the fuck does she think she is?

Carmen smirks, apparently oblivious to the storm raging inside me. "They all want a piece of the empire. If they can't build their own, they'll try to marry into one. Tale as old as time." She shrugs.

There's something in her words that unsettles me. I take another sip of wine to mask the flicker of uncertainty I feel. I shouldn't let this random woman get under my skin. I'm stronger than this. And yet, when it comes to César, I feel like things are so fragile. Breakable.

"You and César...how serious is it?" she asks, eyes sharp despite her gentle tone.

I hesitate. "It's new, but it feels serious."

Carmen nods slowly. "Do you love him?"

The question lands like a stone in my stomach. I'm just starting to get comfortable with the fact I'm dating him. But love? I feel like I've been hit with a ton of bricks. I open my mouth, only to close it again. No doesn't feel right. It feels too much like a lie. So, I say the one thing I can. "I think I could."

"That's dangerous," she says. "Not love, necessarily. But loving a man like him. Power like César's is intoxicating. You feel seen. Wanted. Worshipped. But eventually, you start to wonder if he's in love with you...or with the way you make him feel when you're on his arm, showing you off like a prize."

Her gaze is steady, almost pitying.

I hate how much that resonates.

"You seem like a smart woman," she continues, ignoring —or not noticing—how she's turned my world upside down in a matter of minutes. "But ask yourself—where do you fit in his world? Will he tire of you like he's grown tired of so many before you? You're pretty, but beauty fades. Power doesn't. Not in this world. And I assume you aren't in this world."

I stare at the gold rim of my wine glass, unable to meet her eyes. I just shake my head. For the first time in a long time, I have nothing to say.

Carmen softens, though I'm uncertain if she actually feels bad or simply has me where she wants me. "Forgive me. I've been in your heels. Not with Augustín. He and I ... well, we have our own problems. But he's smart. He knows he needs a woman like me, who can thrive in this dog eat dog world by his side."

I press my lips into a thin line. She's said too much— and yet somehow, it's not enough. I want to ask her why she doesn't think I can be that for César. Why I'm not good enough, but the part of me that still wants to believe in César, so I stay quiet.

"I'm not judging you," Carmen quickly adds, like it will change everything she just said. "But this world? It'll eat you alive if you don't know your worth."

The words echo in my chest long after she turns toward a passing waiter to refresh her champagne.

I murmur an excuse and drift toward the windows, pretending to admire the view. I need space, to get away. Carmen doesn't try to call me back, but I swear I hear her sultry laughter behind me.

Outside, the hotel's gardens are lit up with string

lights, soft glows dancing in the trees. It's beautiful. Serene. Everything I don't feel right now.

Where do I fit in his world?

I think about the way César looks at me, how he touches me like I'm something rare. But I also think about the stares from women in the room, the silent questions behind every polite smile. I think about Carmen's words, still carving themselves into my ribs.

Do I belong here...or am I just convenient? Temporary? Replaceable?

Back home, I was just Lety Zavala. Assistant. Sex worker. Survivor. Now? I'm someone's plus-one in a hotel that smells like money and ambition.

A voice whispers *"Do you really think you're enough for him?"*

It stings. Because I don't know. Not really. And I fucking hate that.

I take a longer sip of wine, willing it to silence the doubt. But it doesn't. It just makes the ache more bearable.

When César returns a little while later, his smile is easy and bright. I paste on one of my own but doubt it's very convincing.

"Everything okay?" he asks, noting the tension in my body. His eyes sweep over me like they can pull every secret out.

"Of course," I lie, just wanting to get through the rest of the night. "Just enjoying the view."

I don't think he believes me. Hell, I'm pretty certain he doesn't believe me, but he also knows this isn't a place to get into it. Instead, he takes my hand and kisses the back of it in a tender gesture tender. Almost perfect.

But all I can think is *Does he love me? Can he learn to love me? Or does he love how I make him feel at this moment?*

These thoughts plague my mind the rest of the night. I do my best to smile when spoken to, laugh when others laugh, eat my food even though I taste nothing.

Even though doubt eats at me from the inside out.

CHAPTER 9

SAY IT FIRST

César

Lety's been quiet most of the evening. Something changed in her when I left her alone to speak with Augustín. Knowing she was uncomfortable, I shouldn't have done that. I get that now, but fuck, it had only been for a couple of minutes. What the fuck did Carmen say to her?

Getting her to talk at the party is damn near impossible now. She evades me around every corner, plastering on a smile as she mingles, though I notice her eyes dart to the exit several times. The only leverage I have is that I brought her here, so she's reliant on me to get her home. But from the looks of it, my girl is ready to run. So, we're back to that.

She still doesn't fucking see it. But she will. Tonight.

Night settles in, and guests begin to disperse, heading home for the night. It's my cue to get the fuck out of here. All I can think about is being alone with Lety. I reach for her hand—relieved when she doesn't pull away from me—

and guide her toward the door. Across the cluster of people, Augustín's eyes find mine among the small crowd gathered to bid their goodbyes. He must see something urgent in my expression because he gives me a subtle nod of farewell. I return it without stopping. As we pass, I notice Lety deliberately avoids Carmen's gaze, and I tighten my grip on her hand, leading her straight to my truck without looking back.

She doesn't speak to me when I open the door for her, nor does she speak when I get in to drive toward her house. The silence is heavy, thick, suffocating. If she thinks this will scare me off, Lety doesn't understand how our arrangement works. She doesn't understand how *I* work.

Lety unfurls her arms from around herself, letting out a shaky breath when we pull up to her house. Her hand slips to the doorhandle, curling around it. "Thank you for tonight. I just—"

I kill the engine and swing my door open before she has a chance to finish whatever damn excuse she's been crafting in her mind since we left the party. My steps are fast, sharp, fueled by frustration and the need to break through whatever wall she's throwing up between us. *Again.* I reach her side and yank open the door. The truck rattles from the force, but I don't care. I lean in, bracing one hand against the frame to keep myself steady. I bite my tongue to keep from saying something I might regret. Lety stares up at me, eyes wide, confusion etched across her face like she's not sure if I'm about to kiss her or explode. I want to do both.

"What are you doing, César? I can open my own door and get into my own house. I don't need your help."

There it is—the fiery attitude I love from her. Most of the night, she's been closed off from me, not meeting my gaze and shying away from my touch. But this anger? I can deal with that.

"I'm keeping my fucking *girlfriend* from running. Again. So, I'm going inside with you. And you're going to tell me exactly what Carmen said to you." I pull back, but only enough to get her out of the car. I offer Lety my hand, but the stubborn woman refuses it, muttering something about "impossible males," before sliding out of the car.

She walks right past me, allowing me to appreciate her ass sway with each step. "How do you know she even said anything to me?" Lety asks, annoyance coloring her words. She rifles through her clutch before pulling out a set of keys to unlock her door. The lock is rusted, sitting slightly askew. I make a mental note to update her security system. I won't rest unless I know she's safe.

Until I can convince her to move in with me, that is.

"Because something changed in you when I came back. It looked like you wanted to bolt," I answer.

Lety snorts but also doesn't deny it. After a moment of struggling with the lock, she pushes open her front door and steps inside. I fall in step behind her, locking it once I'm inside. It occurs to me I've never actually been in Lety's house before. It smells just like her, sugary sweet with a hint of spice. The house is small but well maintained. The living room is decorated with an emerald-green couch, complimented by fuchsia walls with various art and photos adorning it.

All the small trinkets and a half-finished puzzle on the coffee table scream Lety. This is her own personal haven, and she's allowed me—albeit reluctantly—inside of it. I don't take that lightly.

As I'm admiring her space, Lety moves further into the house, down a darkened hallway. I follow, noting the family photos lining the wall. Lety is in the back room, the primary bedroom, kicking off her shoes. Unlike the rest of the house, this room is cluttered with clothes. The bed isn't made, looking freshly slept in, and there's a coffee mug on her bedside table with lipstick stains on the rim.

Lety is mumbling to herself as she kicks her heels off and turns to look at me. There's a wild look in her eyes and I know I'm in for a fight. "This isn't going to work!"

"You yelling at me? I don't know, mi reina. It's getting me all hot and bothered."

Lety hurls a twisted-up shirt at my head. I dodge it and it hits the wall with a dull *thud* before falling back to the floor. "That's not what I meant, and you know it. I can't do this, César. It's not worth fucking up everything we've both built. It's better if we part ways amicably, so we can at least work together civilly. Or hell, I can quit and—"

"You're not fucking quitting," I snarl. "And we're not cutting this off."

"But Carmen said—"

"I don't give a fuck what Carmen said! Augustín just needs to divorce her ass already. I shouldn't have left you alone with her knowing what she's like." I take a deep breath, feeling myself get heated. I need to keep a level-head right now, since Lety certainly won't.

"Wait, what?" Lety scrunches her brow.

I close the space between us, needing to be closer. Lety sucks in a deep breath when I approach, but she doesn't push me away. She's guarded, confused, but doesn't flinch when I reach for her. It's a small crack in her armor I plan to exploit.

"I should've warned you before we left. Carmen's awful." There are harsher things I want to call her, but out of respect for my friend and their kid, I hold back. "She's cold. Self-centered. The kind of person who'll do whatever it takes to get what she wants, even if it means tearing someone else down. She saw a vulnerable moment, and she used it against you. That's the kind of shit she pulls. What did she tell you?"

Lety's hesitant to let me know. She shifts from foot to foot, glancing at the ground. My strong, beautiful woman forgets herself. But she won't. Not after tonight.

My fingers find her chin, coaxing her to meet my eyes. "What did she say?" I ask again.

"That I don't belong in your world. That I'm just another woman in a sea of women before me," she admits, and each word lights a fire within me.

My jaw clenches so hard it hurts.

"Another woman?" I repeat in a low and dangerous tone. "You think I'd bring just *any woman* into my life, into my business, to meet my friends? You think I'd risk everything I've built for something casual?" I scoff, stepping closer, until our bodies are pressed together. She's got nowhere to run. "You don't know me at all if you believe that."

Lety folds her arms like she's trying to hold herself together. "It's not just about that. You'll get tired of me eventually. You'll want someone easier, someone less complicated." She shudders, saying the last word like it's a foul curse.

My chest tightens at her words, and I can't hold back anymore. I'm done with these games. They end here. Now. With her knowing she's mine and I'm hers. "I don't want easy. I want *you*, Lety."

She shakes her head, but her lips tremble, seconds away from losing herself. "You say that now—"

"No," I cut her off, firm but gentle. "Not just *now*. I've

been falling for you since the first time you rolled your eyes at me in that conference room. Since you challenged me instead of catered to my ego. Since I found out what you do in the evenings, and how fucking powerful that makes you."

She huffs out a soft laugh, but I don't let go of her hands.

"You think I'm going to get bored of you?" I scoff, brushing my fingers along her cheek. "Lety, I could spend the rest of my life trying to figure you out and still wake up every morning amazed that you're mine. You're *fire* and *sweetness* and *chaos* all in one, and I've never been more certain of anything than I am of this. I love you."

She flinches like I've struck her, her breath catching. "You can't possibly love me. We just started dating. No one can be certain. I mean, what if these feelings are just lust? What if we are confusing lust and desire with love? What then?"

"I'm in love with you," I repeat, slower this time, letting every word sink in. She needs to hear it. There's no confusion on my part, and soon, there will be none on hers, either. I just need to break through her stubbornness. "Not just the *you* that's sexy as hell when you're mad. Or the *you* who gets on camera and is the fucking most powerful, sexy woman I've ever seen. Not just the *you* I get to kiss or tease or touch. I love *you*. The woman who talks back, who stays late to work and is friends with the janitors. The woman who loves tacos but can't cook to save her life. The woman who walks into a room and makes me feel like I'm home."

Lety's eyes brim with emotion and her lower lip trembles, but she doesn't pull away. She just stands there, breathing hard, trying to keep her walls up. It's a losing battle, though, and I think she knows it. She may be stub-born, but it pales in comparison to my own.

So I push a little more.

"I'm not leaving, mi reina. I'm not going anywhere. I don't give a shit what Carmen said. I don't care what doubts are in your head. You want to fight? I'll fight. You want to push me away? Fine, push. But I'm still going to be right here, loving you like it's the only damn thing that matters. Because it is."

She swallows hard, blinking rapidly, and I can practi-cally see the moment her defenses start to crumble. It's glorious. Beautiful. Just like her.

I lower myself, pressing my forehead to hers. Lety exhales, eyes fluttering close. She reaches up to grip my arms, as if trying to keep herself steady. That's what I want to be for her. Her anchor in a storm when she needs it.

"You are not just another woman. You're *the* woman. Mine."

Her hands tighten around my arms, and when she finally meets my eyes, I see it—that flicker of belief. There's war still raging inside her, yes, but also hope.

And hope is all I need.

I kiss her. Because she's done hearing words. She needs to see and feel them.

Her lips move in time with mine, and I feel her worries and fears start to fall away. I gather her in my arms, and she yelps as I pick her up. "César! What are you doing?" Her voice is breathless, unbridled desire coating her words.

I smirk. "I'm taking my girl to bed, so I can show her just how serious I am."

"Oh. Okay, yeah." She's flustered. It's cute.

I've never made love to a woman before. I've fucked

plenty. Had passionate sex. Rough sex. Many different types. But never love. I make sure to show it in every move I make.

In the way that I strip her of her clothes, kissing down her collarbone, tasting the sweetness of her skin. The little breathy moans she makes spur me on. I unclasp her bra, freeing her glorious tits from their confines, and immediately take her nipple into my mouth.

"Baby," she moans.

It's music to my fucking ears.

I don't remember how the rest of our clothes fell to the floor or who took them off. I'm consumed by the woman underneath me. I break down each of her walls with a kiss, savoring the way she tastes on my tongue. Perfect. It feels like the start of forever.

And then I'm inside of her. I bury my cock deep within her, claiming her from the inside out.

"You. Are. Mine," I moan in her ear between thrusts. Each movement is a claiming and an undoing. But also a beginning.

The beginning of us.

I move faster, more urgently. The bed creaks under our weight, and Lety arches her back off the mattress.

"César, please," she moans. She's close. I feel it. But so am I.

"Tell me you're mine." I press the pad of my thumb down on her clit and still.

She whines, trying to grind down to reach her release, but I pull my hand back. "Say it. Say you're mine, and I'll let you come, mi reina."

"Fuck, okay. Okay, I'm yours, César. I swear to God if you make me regret this, I will kill you. I—Ah!" Her words end in a breathy moan as my finger finds her clit once again.

Her body tenses before her orgasm rips through her, and she's coming for my cock. I follow close behind, filling her. Claiming her once and for all. She will never have to question my feelings for her. And if she does, I'll simply show her again and again.

But there's no running. Because I will always chase her. And if she wants to run away to a cabin like she told me in the private chat, then I'll run away with her.

After we clean up, we lay in her bed, her head resting against my chest.

"I love you, Lety," I murmur, needing her to hear again.

She doesn't speak at first, just traces circles around my chest with her finger. Finally, she looks up at me. The fear from earlier doesn't linger. Just peace. Acceptance. "Remember what I said, César. Break my heart and I will kill you. Or make your life hell. I have all your passwords, you know."

I can't help but laugh. My evil, vengeful girl. I got a lifetime of this. I just hope it will be enough. "Noted, mi reina. I'll protect your heart."

I realize that she hasn't said "I love you" back. That's okay. I can be patient. I can wait just a little longer for her to say it back.

Because one day she will.

EPILOGUE - NEXT VALENTINE'S DAY

Lety

Valentine's Day still sucks, but I guess this year it's tolerable. I had wanted to do business as usual, but as I was getting ready to work this morning—using the spare bathroom because our primary bathroom is undergoing renovations—César popped his head in, buttoning up his shirt. He had told me not to go into work, treating Valentine's Day like it's freaking Christmas and not some overly priced commercial holiday.

"And miss hearing about Melanie's fake boyfriend? Not a chance, buddy," I had said, adding a few curls to my hair.

"They broke up," he said casually, like he didn't just drop a steaming cup of piping hot tea.

I had slammed the curling wand on the counter, whirling on him. "When? How the hell do you know?"

César just shrugged, and for all his strengths, he is, unfortunately, still a man, so naturally he gave me little information other than she was crying in his office one morning and he had to send her home.

Reluctantly, I agreed to stay home, promising not to leave the house—*our* house. It's still feels so strange to say that. I'm living with my boyfriend. More surprisingly, I love it. I had thought moving in with César would steal away some of my independence, but it hasn't. If anything, it's not only strengthened our relationship, but strengthened me as a person. If someone would have said that to me last Valentine's Day, I would have called them delusional.

It still feels like a fantasy. One I never have to wake up from.

Even though I agreed to stay home, César still claimed he needed to leave. He didn't say he had to go into work, but he also didn't tell me what he was scheming. And he's definitely scheming something. It's my man's favorite day of the year. Despite my shitty attitude toward Valentine's Day, I have to admit, even I'm a little excited for what he's planning.

Just a little.

With nothing else pressing this morning, I'm considering batching some content for DesireDen. The idea both excites and unsettles me. Even though César said he was okay with me keeping the account, a part of me still doesn't believe him. He's a possessive man—fiercely so—and I've been waiting for the moment that possessiveness would spill over into jealousy.

It never made sense to me that he'd be fine with me undressing for the camera, touching myself for an audience of faceless subscribers. The thought alone used to make my heart race—not with desire, but with dread. I kept expecting the other shoe to drop. For him to slam the door shut on this part of my life. For the fights to start. For the inevitable choice: give up the thing that makes me feel powerful and in control of my body or give up the man who makes me feel seen and wanted in a completely different way.

And yet, that moment never came. No angry ultimatums. No icy silence. Just his word and the terrifying possibility that he might actually mean it. Even when I tried to guilt trip myself into deleting my account, César would adamantly refuse, knowing it wasn't what I truly wanted.

I loved this man. Body and soul. I think he knows it; I just haven't told him that yet. But I will. Today. It seems like a fitting day to make proclamations of love. Consider me in the spirit.

The doorbell rings, pulling me from my thoughts. I frown as I realize I'm not expecting anyone and pull my phone out to check the camera—something César insisted we need for surveillance. I actually sort of love it.

My screen fills with an array of colorful flowers, and a short, skinny man struggling to hold the arrangement nearly half his size. Not wanting him to keel over and ruin what I suspect to be mine, I hurry to answer the door. The relief in his eyes is almost comical when he sees me.

"Are you Ms. Zavala?" the man asks, before promptly sneezing into his arm. "Sorry, flowers give me the worst allergies."

"Seems to me you're in the wrong business then."

The man just shrugs. "So, are you Ms. Zavala? These are getting heavy."

"Oh, yeah. That's me." I go to take the arrangement from him, and he hands it over, along with a pink card. He doesn't bother saying bye before taking off toward his white van with "Flowers For All Occasions" in bright, bubbly letters on the side.

Using my hip to close the front door, I take the giant

assortment inside and head for the kitchen. I still stand by what I said the first time I ever saw this house; it's so damn big. But we have somehow managed to fill the space, exchanging the model house it once looked like for a homier space.

I place the vase in the center of our dining room table, turning it until it's just right. I adjust the flowers slightly—spreading the petals, fluffing a few stems—until the bouquet looks full and inviting.

He got my favorite flowers, peonies and hydrangeas. I didn't even know I had favorite flowers until I started dating him. Who knew?

The card is still in my hand. The outside is pink with "mi reina" printed in cursive on the front. My heart swells as I open the note, racing to read every word. There's not much to it.

Be ready in an hour. Wear that red dress I like.

An hour? This man will be the death of me with his bizarre deadlines and cryptic messages. Though I can't deny the thrill spreading through my body.

Oh, he's definitely up to something.

Not wanting to waste any more precious time, I rush to our bedroom on the second floor. Luckily, my hair and makeup are mostly done from this morning. The red dress in question hangs in the back of my closet. I strip down to my panties and bra before gently taking the dress off the hanger and sliding it on my body. It's a tight fit, more so than usual. It's true what they say about gaining weight in a happy relationship. It would be more if not for the amazing—and sweaty—sex we have almost nightly.

Zipping up the dress took a Herculean effort, and by the time I'm done, I'm panting as if I just went for a morning jog. Once my breathing is normal, I head to the spare bathroom to touch up my hair and makeup, taking a quick photo of myself to send to César.

He responds not even a minute later.

> Fucking beautiful. I'm coming to get
> you now.

My body buzzes with excitement. I feel giddy, like a teenager waiting for their prom date. Is this how other people feel on Valentine's Day? I guess I understand the hype now.

Not knowing how far away he is, I grab matching red heels and add the diamond earrings he bought me last month for my birthday. One last look in the mirror, and I'm definitely feeling myself. I feel hot. I would definitely fuck myself.

A bell chimes from downstairs, signaling the front door has opened. My heart stumbles in my chest, and it takes every ounce of restraint I have not to race to slide down the banister like a lovesick puppy. I force myself to take the stairs like an adult—slow, measured steps—but the second I spot César, the breath catches in my throat. It's only been a few hours since I last saw him, yet I ached for this. For him. Just the sight of him settles something deep inside me. With him, I feel safe. Whole. Like I've finally found home.

Sensing me staring at him, César turns, lips lifting into the smile he reserves solely for me. It's full of love and adoration, something that has taken me far too long to accept. But now that I have, it's my favorite thing to see.

"Get down here so I can admire you properly."

At his command, I take the last few steps and make my way across the living room until I'm standing a few feet in front of him. His eyes roam my body, slowly moving from my face, all the way down to my toes and back up again. His eyes darken, tension hanging heavy between us. Will it always be like this? Wanting to rip each other's clothes off and fuck like rabbits?

God, I hope so.

César closes the distance between us, resting his hand on my hip. That small gesture sends tremors and heat racing down my spine. My body scorches from his touch. "A fucking vision. That's what you are, Lety. I'm so damn lucky."

"Yes, you are," I say, far too breathlessly to sound unaffected by his words.

He smirks, knowing exactly what he does to me. "Did you like the flowers?"

And because I'm a brat, I say, "I did, but I was disappointed there wasn't any chocolate. Don't they kind of go together?"

"Oh, there'll be chocolate, mi reina. But not until tonight, when I can lick it off that sexy body."

His words heat my core, and my cheeks flush. The asshole just laughs, clearly liking me wound up for him.

"Do you want to know what I have planned for us?" he asks, brushing a loose strand of hair out of my face.

"I do," I whisper, distracted by the way he licks his lips as he takes me in.

"I went all out for Valentine's Day. I'm certain you'll hate every moment of it," he teases.

I'm salivating at the mouth to know. "Tell me."

"I'm taking you to an overpriced restaurant downtown."

"Mm, a traditional man. I like it. Keep going."

"Dessert will obviously have to come next."

"Obviously. Bonus points if it's chocolate-covered strawberries."

"And then..." He hums, closing the gap between us. He rests his free hand on the curve of my ass, squeezing lightly. I let out an involuntary groan. "And then I'm taking you to the cabin I just bought."

My brow furrows. Out of everything I thought he'd say, I didn't imagine that. "You bought a cabin?"

"For us." He nods like it's a normal thing to do. His eyes then pierce mine, looking into my soul. "Because you once told me you wish you had an escape sometimes. A place where you could go and forget the world when you felt like running. So, mi reina, if you ever feel the need to run, you have somewhere to go. And I swear I'll be right behind you. Forever. You'll never be alone."

Tears sting my eyes as a tidal wave of emotions crashes over me, nearly stealing my breath. How long have I been aching for this—for someone to truly see me? The raw, messy, complicated parts of me. The not-so-pretty parts. Not just tolerate them but accept them. Embrace them. I've spent so long bracing for rejection, ready to run the moment I felt too exposed. But César? He doesn't flinch. He doesn't look at me like I'm too much. Like I'm not enough. He sees straight through to the heart of me and doesn't turn away.

Instead, he bought us a place to run away to together. Always together.

"I love you." The words are out before I can stop them.

César's hand, which had moved to play with my hair, freezes and his body tenses.

This is not how I wanted to tell him. There was supposed to be a grand gesture. After dinner, under the stars. Something. Not here in the middle of the living room with tears in my eyes.

After what feels like an eternity, César finally speaks. "Say it again."

This time, I'm prepared. I look directly into his eyes, seeing him like he sees me. "I love you, César. I have for a while now. You've made me feel loved, seen, safe. The only place I want to run to is your arms every night. I love you, baby."

I want to scream and shout it now that the words are out in the open. They don't feel adequate enough for how I feel, and I wonder if this is how he felt the first time he said it.

Then César grabs my face between his hands and crashes us together. His lips meet mine in a searing kiss I feel all the way down to my bones. He kisses me like I'm his life force. The only thing keeping him alive. I cling to him. Desperate. Needing him not only to hear the words, but feel them, too.

"Say it one more time," he murmurs against my lips. "Please, Lety."

This time, it's my turn to caress his cheek, feeling the rough stubble on my palm. "I love you, César Estrada."

"And I love you, mi reina. I love you so fucking much."

"Happy Valentine's Day, baby," I say through my tears.

"Happy Valentine's Day, Lety."

He then kisses me like a promise—slow, deep, and full of everything we've survived to get here. In his arms, I'm not just loved. I'm seen, wanted, and cherished. I'm his in every aspect of the word. In every way a person can be.

And for the first time in a long time, I know I'm exactly where I'm meant to be.

Halloween is a time for candy, costumes, and fun.

For Augustín Cisneros, it's a time to rid himself of the haunting memory of his vicious ex.

Marrying Carmen had been a mistake. Sure, on paper they'd worked, but he's had enough of her cold, materialistic ways. When she attempts to take his assets in the divorce proceedings, he's ready to fight fire with fire—all while keeping his son far removed from the drama and in the comforting arms of their new live-in nanny, Elena Cantu.

Elena has always wanted a family of her own, but until that day comes, she's content with her job as a nanny. What she didn't expect was the fierce attraction she feels for her boss—or that their business relationship would become something more. But when Carmen begins threatening Augustín with a full custody battle over his son, Elena must decide if she's willing to stand by his side...or if their relationship is doomed before it even begins.

Anastasia Dean is a pen name for Tati B. Alvarez. She lives in Austin, Texas, where she spends most days lost in her own head, creating stories. When she is not writing, you can find her vacationing at Disney World.